Traitor
– in the –
Tower

Trailblazer Books

*Hero Tales: A Family Treasury of True Stories
From the Lives of Christian Heroes* (Volumes I, II, III, & IV)

---

*Curriculum guide available.
Written by Julia Pferdehirt with Dave & Neta Jackson.   02C

Traitor
– in the –
Tower

Dave & Neta Jackson

Story illustrations by
Julian Jackson

BETHANY HOUSE PUBLISHERS
MINNEAPOLIS, MINNESOTA 55438

Traitor in the Tower
Copyright © 1997
Dave and Neta Jackson

Illustrations © 1997
Bethany House Publishers

Story illustrations by Julian Jackson
Cover design and illustration by Catherine Reishus McLaughlin

Scripture quotations are from the King James Version of the Bible.

Published by Bethany House Publishers
A Ministry of Bethany Fellowship International
11400 Hampshire Avenue South
Minneapolis, Minnesota 55438
www.bethanyhouse.com

Printed in the United States of America by
Bethany Press International, Minneapolis, Minnesota 55438

Library of Congress Cataloging-in-Publication Data

Jackson, Dave
    Traitor in the tower : John Bunyan / Dave and Neta Jackson ; text illustrations by Julian Jackson.
        p.   cm. — (Trailblazer books ; #22)
    Includes bibliographical references (p.).
    Summary: In 1660, after his father is imprisoned in the Tower of London, Richard Winslow goes to stay with his uncle who is in charge of the Gedford jail and there meets and is helped by the Puritan preacher John Bunyan, author of Pilgrim's Progress.
    ISBN 1–55661–741–0
    1. Bunyan, John, 1628–1688—Junvenile fiction. [1. Bunyan, Joh, 1628–1688—Fiction. 2. Puritans—Fiction. 3. Great Britain—History—Charles II, 1660–1685—Fiction. 4. Christian life—Fiction.] I. Jackson, Neta. II. Jackosn, Julian, ill. III. Title. III. Series: Jackson, Dave. Trailblazer books.
PZ7.J132418Th   1996
[Fic]—dc21   96–45854
                                                                    CIP
                                                                    AC

The Winslows of this story are fictional, as are Elder Barnabas of the secret London church and John White's wife, whom we called Agnes. All other named characters and events in this story are real. John White served as the under-jailer at the Bedford jail during the time when John Bunyan was imprisoned there. Not only did White nearly lose his position because of the liberties he granted Bunyan, but he was so strongly influenced by Bunyan's witness that he got in trouble for refusing to pay the state church tax.

Also, the details surrounding Bunyan's imprisonment were somewhat more complex than we were able to portray in this book.

The stories told by John Bunyan are adaptations of his allegory *Pilgrim's Progress*.

Find us on the Web at . . .

trailblazerbooks.com

- Meet the authors.

- Read the first chapter of each book—with the pictures.

- Track the Trailblazers around the world on a map.

- Use the historical timeline to find out what other important events were happening in the world at the time of each Trailblazer story.

- Discover how the authors research their books and link to some of the same sources they used where you can learn more about these heroes.

- Write to the authors.

- Explore frequently asked questions about the Trailblazer books and being writers.

Just point your browser to http://www.trailblazerbooks.com

CONTENTS

DAVE AND NETA JACKSON are a full-time husband/wife writing team who have authored and coauthored many books on marriage and family, the church, relationships, and other subjects. Their books for children include the TRAILBLAZER series and *Hero Tales* Volumes I, II, and III. The Jacksons have two married children, Julian and Rachel, and make their home in Evanston, Illinois.

Chapter 1

The Midnight Raid

BANG! BANG! BANG!
The crashing yanked Richard Winslow out of a sound sleep. Or was he still dreaming? Was he in a castle with the enemy at the gate? No. As his wits came to him, he realized that he was in his own bedroom, and the banging and yelling came from the front door of his house just below his bedroom.

Bang! Bang! Bang! "Open up in the name of the king!"

A flickering yellow light came through Richard's window and danced on the ceiling of his room. Then he heard his father calling out for the butler. "Walter! Walter—

what's happening? Who's at the door? Someone light a candle."

Richard jumped out of bed as he heard his father run past his door and scramble down the stairs. Richard followed partway down the stairs in time to see his father open the heavy front door of their London house.

In barged two of the king's men with swords drawn.

As Richard hesitated on the landing of the stairway, he could see other soldiers outside. One had a torch in his hand, and its light cast a flickering glow into the dim hallway.

"I am the captain of the king's guard," barked the older of the two soldiers inside the house. "Is this the home of Obadiah Winslow? Are you Winslow?" He took a threatening step toward Richard's father.

"It is, and I am," said Mr. Winslow as he pushed his nightcap back on his head and stood up straighter. But it was hard to appear as a dignified gentleman in a wrinkled nightshirt and bare feet.

"Who else lives in this house?" demanded the captain as he ducked down to peer up the dark stairway toward where Richard crouched on the landing. Richard crept back from the edge and tried to make himself invisible.

Obadiah Winslow also glanced up the stairs, then stammered, "J-just my family—my wife and children."

"Is that all?" The soldier looked toward the back of the hall. "What about back there?"

"Well, there's the maid . . . and the butler," Mr.

Winslow said as the side door swung open and the old butler tottered into the hall holding a candle high with one hand. The old man's mouth hung open, and in the dim glow of the candlelight he appeared dazed.

"Who are these people?" he muttered. "I am the butler here, and I have not given you permission to enter this—"

"Silence, old man!" shouted the captain. "This is none of your business." He turned back to Richard's father. "Obadiah Winslow, I arrest you in the name of the crown for high treason. You will come with us."

"Treason! B-but this cannot be," stammered Obadiah. "I have done nothing wrong. Who is making these outrageous charges? What led to them?"

"I cannot say," said the captain. He tilted his head back and looked down his nose at his prisoner. "I am neither judge nor prosecutor. However, I do recall that you had a rather long and close association with that traitor, Oliver Cromwell. You were his assistant secretary, weren't you?" The captain smiled slyly.

Shock spread across Obadiah's face. "W-why, yes. But, but—he died in 1658, over two years ago, before young King Charles returned to England. Besides," said Richard's father, trying to regain some control over the situation, "I thought that the king granted amnesty to anyone associated with Cromwell. He promised it in his Declaration of Breda. Everyone knows that."

"What the king promised or didn't promise is none of my business," said the soldier. "The king *is* the king, after all." The captain slid his sword back into its scabbard and looked Richard's father up and down. "You're a sorry sight to be going to the Tower," he snarled. "Go put on some clothes, but make it quick. We don't have all night."

Obadiah sucked in his breath. "The Tower? Why the Tower?" But seeing that he could not evade the king's soldiers, Obadiah Winslow took a candlestick off the mantel, lit it off the butler's candle, and trudged up the stairs. When he got to the landing on which Richard crouched, he put his hand on the boy's shoulder and said, "Come along, son."

The bewildered butler was left downstairs facing the soldiers—as though such a feeble old man could stop them from invading the Winslow house any farther.

Upstairs, behind closed doors, Richard's mother, Eunice, and his three younger sisters pelted Obadiah with anxious questions. On the far side of the room, Molly, the maid, stood holding her skirt up to her mouth as she cried bitterly.

"Just calm down," Mr. Winslow said firmly. "I don't know what's happening. It's some mix-up about Cromwell. But before the king was even allowed back into England, he promised freedom to all his enemies—though I have never considered myself an enemy of the crown. I'm sure I'll be released in the morning as soon as we get this mess sorted out. Don't worry about me. Just calm down and put yourselves back to bed."

Sensing the fear in their mother, the girls began to cry as they clung to their mother's nightdress. The whole thing seemed like a nightmare—the banging on the door, soldiers arresting their father.

Richard found that he was shivering uncontrollably even though he didn't feel cold, but he gritted his teeth and refused to cry. He was tall for twelve, with a shock of dark, wavy hair that would have gone to curls had he let it grow long. His face was square with a strong jaw for his age. He watched nervously as his father pulled on his trousers and buckled his shoes.

"Keep a stiff upper lip," his father said as he patted him on the shoulder. Richard knew that meant he wasn't to cry; it would only upset his sisters even more.

Once his father had been taken away by the soldiers, Richard's three weeping sisters crawled into bed with their mother, but Richard was much too old for that. He went back to his own room.

The June night was warm, but his bed felt cold, and he continued to shiver. It all seemed so unreal. Maybe none of it had happened; it was nothing more than a bad dream. But no . . . dreams wandered from one scene to another, and even in the most vivid dreams there were always things that didn't fit—like the stairs turning into a waterfall.

But the midnight raid had been one continuous sequence, and the only thing that didn't make sense was *why*. Why had soldiers come for his father? It made no sense.

It was true that his father had worked closely with Oliver Cromwell as he led his armies against old King Charles. And after the king had been defeated and executed, Obadiah Winslow had assisted Cromwell when he ruled England for five years as the "Lord Protector." But all that was in the past. Cromwell had died, and now Charles II, as he was being called, had been brought back from Europe to sit on the throne.

All the old quarrels were supposedly put to rest, everyone pardoned for earlier allegiances. It had all been politics, and politics made enemies, but who could tell right from wrong?

So why *had* his father been arrested?

Richard thought about the Tower with a shudder. The Tower of London was about two and a half miles down the Thames River, across London from where he lived. He had been by it several times. There were two high stone walls—one inside the other—that surrounded a tall, square "keep" with turrets on each of the four corners. This structure was "the Tower." Earlier, it had been used as a castle by the king or queen—something no enemy could invade. However, when someone realized that invaders could not enter and prisoners could not escape, it became a prison. But it was not a prison for common thieves and mischief makers. This prison housed only major criminals and enemies of the king. Very few prisoners who went through its gates came out alive.

Richard moaned and pulled the covers over his head.

At some point he must have fallen asleep, because the events of the midnight raid merged into a dream . . . or nightmare, as it became. The king's soldiers were after him, but the faster he tried to run, the more difficult it was to move his feet. The street seemed to turn into a muddy field, and with every step his boots gathered more mud until his feet were so heavy that he could hardly pick them up. He became exhausted, and the soldiers were just about to grab him when he finally woke up.

It was morning. Birds were chirping and the fishmonger was coming down the street calling out, "Eels, two a penny! Fresh eels! Get 'em now or let 'em go! Salted herring. You need it? I got it!"

Richard got out of bed and pulled a blanket with him, wrapping it around his shoulders as he shuffled to the small window overlooking the street below. As his blue eyes gazed down, the night's horrors came back to him: His father had been arrested and taken to the Tower!

Quickly, he threw on his clothes and ran downstairs. "Has my father come home?" he blurted to Walter as he burst into the kitchen.

"No, Master Richard," Walter said as he set down the coal bucket by the open fireplace. "We haven't seen a whisker of him."

"I'm going out to see what I can learn," announced Richard.

"Oh no. You mustn't. After last night, it's not safe," clucked Molly, pulling a large loaf of fresh bread out of the oven.

The Winslow family did not have a large household staff—only Walter, who was called the butler, but he did many other chores as well, and Molly, who also served as a cook and nurse for the children when necessary. In spite of Obadiah Winslow's close association with the former head of the English government, the family was not wealthy. So they made do with what they had.

Richard looked at Molly as she set the fresh bread on the table. "Can I have some bread and butter?" he asked.

"Certainly, but I don't think your mother would want you running around in the streets."

Richard cut a thick slice of the hot bread and spread butter on it. The butter melted immediately and smelled delicious. He didn't want to argue with Molly. She'd just call his mother, and then he would have to stay home. So he took such an enormous bite that no one could have understood him when he mumbled, "I won't be gone long," and rushed out the back door.

He ran down the alley, then ducked between two buildings and came out onto the street. The day was already warm. Not far away, the leaves on the trees around Westminster Abbey, the great church, still had the yellowish green of new growth. But Richard had no sooner started to enjoy the beauty of the day when his thoughts slammed against the memory of his father's arrest.

Westminster Abbey . . . Oliver Cromwell was

buried there, inside the stone cathedral. The boy clenched his fists angrily. His father was not a traitor for having worked for Cromwell! Richard wished the old man were still around to explain to the king or the judge or the soldiers that his father was a good man.

As Richard approached Westminster Hall, he became aware of a crowd, restless and murmuring. The faint smell of something musty and old wafted on the morning breeze. He stopped in shock.

Hanging from a tall pole was a dark and twisted shape wrapped in what seemed to be old clothes. It looked like a skeletal corpse had been hung from a gallows. Richard pushed his way through the crowd until he could read a sign mounted on top of the pole: "Here hangs the remains of Oliver Cromwell, guilty of treason. Let all traitors beware! This will happen to you!"

Horrified, Richard backed out of the crowd and tripped over a stone and fell. But the jolt of hitting the ground was not nearly as great as what he had seen. Scrambling to his feet in panic, he ran for home.

Chapter 2

Escape From London

RICHARD RAN INTO HIS HOUSE yelling, "Mother! Mother! They've hung Oliver Cromwell!" He skidded to a stop in the kitchen where his mother, sisters, and the butler and maid were eating breakfast.

Normally, Molly served breakfast to the family on trays in their bedrooms. But given the frightening events of the night before, everyone had gathered in the kitchen.

"What do you mean?" said Eunice Winslow. "Cromwell's been dead for over two years. No one hung him. He died a natural death, and we all know that his body is buried in the tomb at Westminster. So sit down, catch your breath, and speak sensibly."

"But they did hang him!" insisted Richard. He did not sit down but stood behind a chair, gripping its back and nervously tipping it back and forth as though it were the handle of a pump. "They hanged him! I saw it myself in front of Westminster Abbey. He's still there."

"Possibly," offered Walter in a voice tuned for speaking to a child much younger than Richard. "Perhaps what you saw was an *effigy*. Maybe someone made a dummy and dressed it up to look like Lord Cromwell. Could that have been it, Master Richard?"

"I'm not a baby," protested Richard, objecting to Walter's tone of voice. "Do dummies smell like... like... ? I found an old dead cat once. I know what *dead* smells like. He was dead! I could see his skull with brownish skin stretched over it. There were eyeholes, and yellow teeth, and he had long, stringy gray hair just like when he was alive. *Someone took him out of the tomb and hung him up.*"

"Eeaah," said Anne, his oldest sister, making a sick face.

But Richard looked around at the unbelieving adults. "Go see for yourself. There was a whole crowd of people gathered there. You can ask anyone."

Suddenly, the expression on his mother's face changed from disbelief to concern. "What else was happening?" she asked. "Were there any soldiers about?"

"No, no soldiers. But there was a sign on the pole.
It said, 'Here hangs the remains of Oliver Cromwell,

guilty of treason.' " He frowned as he tried to remember. " 'Traitors beware!' or something like that."

No one spoke for almost a minute. Then Eunice Winslow said gravely, "If this is true, Richard, then what happened to your father last night is far more serious than I realized. If the winds of politics have changed again, we may no longer be safe."

"What's going to happen to Papa?" wailed Chelsea, Richard's middle sister. A whimper escaped her throat, and her face screwed up as she began to cry.

"We don't know yet," said Mrs. Winslow soothingly, brushing her daughter's hair out of her eyes. "But one thing is certain. We must not cause Papa greater concern by having to worry about us. I think we'd better get out of London."

"Out of London?" said Richard. His mind swirled. He wasn't sure he wanted to leave this familiar house and his friends. "But... where will we go?"

"I don't know," said his mother as she looked back and forth between Walter and Molly. "Maybe... maybe we could go to our relatives in Scotland. I'm sure they would be glad for a visit. And then when this thing blows over we'll come back." She smiled bravely at the young girls.

"But that would take over two weeks, madam," said Walter with a knowing air.

"Only if we go by land. By ship we should arrive in less than a week."

"A ship! We're going by sea?" Richard felt a thrill of excitement—then immediately felt guilty. What about Papa? They couldn't just leave him behind in the Tower.

"Shall I begin packing, ma'am?" asked Molly.

"Yes, if you would, please."

"Then I'll get the carriage prepared," offered Walter.

"I don't think we should take our own carriage," said Mrs. Winslow. "It might attract too much attention. People recognize it, you know. We'll hire a public carriage, but not until dark. What I'd like you to do, Walter, is go down to the docks and arrange passage for us. Make sure it is on a decent ship and that we can board tonight after dark. We don't want to be seen by any more people than is necessary."

"Very well, madam," said Walter.

"And Walter," continued Mrs. Winslow, "when you come back, I want you to shut up the house as though we have gone away on holiday. I think that would be best. I want Molly to come with us, but will you stay here to look after things?"

As the family servant, Walter never objected to the instructions given him, but he often let his opinion be known by a smile if he approved, or by raising an eyebrow or straightening his neck if he disapproved. This time, he both straightened his neck and raised his eyebrow, but Mrs. Winslow continued without hesitation. "I want you to enter and leave only through the back, Walter. And light no candles or lamps in the front part of the house at night. We want everyone to think we are gone. However, someone needs to remain here in case—" she paused and glanced at the children— "for *when* Obadiah is re-leased."

Richard noticed her hesitation and realized that his mother feared the worst: Obadiah Winslow might *not* come home from the Tower.

They worked all day packing and preparing the house for their absence. Supper was cold—just bread and cheese, some apples, and cider. At the table, Mrs. Winslow finally spoke the thought that had been on everyone's mind. "I hate for us to all be so far away from Obadiah. What if he needs us?"

"*I* will be here, Mrs. Winslow," said Walter. He sounded hurt and indignant.

"I know, I know, Walter, but I don't think you could get in to visit him. Sometimes they admit only immediate family members."

The thought crossed Richard's mind that he could stay. Possibly he could get in to see his father. But if he stayed, he would miss traveling by ship to Scotland. Once, when he was about seven years old, his father had taken him on board a ship that was anchored in the Thames. Ever since, he had dreamed of traveling by sea! But a sea voyage without his father—with his father in *danger*—felt wrong, somehow. No, he chided himself, helping his father was the greater necessity.

"What about me, Mother?" he finally said quietly.

Mrs. Winslow looked at him thoughtfully. Then, "No, son. I couldn't risk your staying in London. That would be unwise."

"Well then," Richard thought for a moment, "what

if I went to stay with Uncle John and Aunt Agnes in Bedford? I'd be safe there, and I could come back to London and visit Father when things are safer."

At first, Mrs. Winslow's head shook firmly from side to side. But then it slowed, and thoughtful lines appeared in her brow as she reconsidered. "Possibly. Bedford is only about fifty miles northwest of London, and John White is not one of the gentry. I doubt that anyone is paying any attention to John and Agnes." She put the palms of her hands to her cheeks, thinking aloud. "I could take the whole family there, but that would be too obvious. However, you—I suppose you would be safe. But I don't know about you trying to come back to London. That could be too risky."

Richard swallowed. On the one hand, he wanted to travel on board the ship with his mother and sisters. But staying with his uncle and aunt would be almost like being on his own. He felt pulled both ways. His father needed a family member near, and he was the oldest. It was a grave responsibility... was he brave enough to take it?

"Let me stay with Uncle John and Aunt Agnes," he finally said in his calmest, most adult-like manner. "I'll be careful."

Finally, it was settled. Mrs. Winslow and the girls would go to the ship during the night, and he would catch the next day's mail stage for Bedford. His mother went to her room to write a letter for him to take to his uncle explaining the danger and also the need for a family member to remain as close to London as possible.

It was dark when Mrs. Winslow, the girls, and Molly got into the carriage to be taken to the dock. Walter went with them for protection and to handle the luggage. But he would return as soon as the family was aboard ship.

Richard went back into the dark house and was immediately struck with how gloomy and empty the place seemed. He did not envy Walter's staying there alone. The chaos of the night before haunted him. He remembered vividly being rudely awakened when the soldiers banged on the door and arrested his father. In such a short time his whole life had turned upside down. Now he was going away to a strange town to stay with relatives he had not seen for several years. It was exciting... and scary.

The next morning Walter took Richard to catch the mail coach to Bedford at a pub on the north side of London. To get there, they again traveled by rented carriage. Richard knew that Walter disapproved of the plan because all morning he had said no more than necessary.

"What's the matter?" Richard finally asked as they jostled along through the streets of London.

"Nothing, Master Richard," grumbled the old man. "It's just... it seems to me that a boy of your age ought to be with his mother. I don't know what this new generation is coming to. This certainly would not have happened when I was your age, at least not among respectable people."

Richard knew that Walter's little comment about "respectable people" was intended to scold him for being so brash. He didn't know how to respond. He wasn't going off to his uncle's because he thought he was such a big shot. It was just the necessity of the situation.

He tilted his chin, trying to sound confident. "Things are different now, Walter. Lots of things are different. Nothing seems safe. Who knows what tomorrow will bring? I must do what I can." He didn't mean to be rude. But the midnight raid by the soldiers had changed everything—and he was scared.

Chapter 3

The Jail Keeper

T HE NEXT AFTERNOON as the mail coach plowed through the muddy rural roads, Richard braced himself and stared straight ahead at the man in a powdered wig who sat in the seat across from him. Richard had never experienced such a rough ride. Foot-deep ruts created by heavy summer rains yanked the coach's wheels this way and that with no warning.

More than once Richard had been looking out the window at the lush green countryside when the coach had lurched so violently that his chin had smashed onto the windowsill. And now, to make matters worse, the constant jostling had caused him to feel sick to his stomach.

He had heard people speak of seasickness. Was this how his mother and sisters were feeling on the ship to Scotland?

But the thought of them so far away while he was becoming sicker by the moment made him feel worse rather than better. If there ever was a time to be home in your own bed with people who loved and cared for you, it was when you were sick. Richard was trying to be a man, to do the grown-up thing—but right now all he wanted was his mother to soothe his head with a cool, damp cloth.

He broke into a sweat and clenched his lips tightly together. He would not throw up. Whatever happened, he would not let himself throw up on the coach!

"What's the matter, lad?" said the man across from Richard. "You look a little green around the gills. Do you want me to signal the driver to stop?"

Richard didn't dare open his mouth. He shook his head, no. But even that extra movement brought another wave of dizziness.

The man across from him looked out the window and then turned back to Richard. "Just you hang on a bit longer. We'll be in Bedford soon. Then you can take a break."

Bedford. The trip was almost over. Nearly two days on the road would wear anyone out. But these last couple hours—ever since they had turned off the Great North Road—traveling had been torture.

Richard couldn't wait to put his feet on solid ground again.

Bedford was a sleepy town, the county seat of Bedfordshire. Richard was grateful when the road became smoother and he noticed that he was riding past houses. For the most part, they were small townhouses with partially exposed timbers at the corners and crossing as braces. Between them brick and stone was plastered as a rough stucco. The roofs of the buildings were generally thatch, though some buildings had red tile roofs.

But the thing that amazed Richard was that behind the rows of houses that lined the streets, there were open grain fields and orchards as though the houses made a picket fence around the field in the center of each large block. This was so different than London where, except for the gardens of the very rich, buildings covered every inch of space not taken up by the narrow streets.

Richard stared out of the window as he rode by a large church.

"That's Saint Mary's Church," offered the man sitting across from Richard. "We'll be crossing the Ouse River in a moment. Then I'll be home, and you, my young traveler, can take a break."

"Oh, this is as far as I am going, too," said Richard. "Do you live in Bedford?"

"I most certainly do. I am Edmund Wylde, the

sheriff of Bedfordshire. So you better mind the law, young man." But his proud smile indicated that he was not issuing a threat. The man turned and looked out the window. "Oh, here we go, across Great Bridge. Now, don't you think it is a fine structure for a small town like this?"

Richard looked out as the wheels of the coach clattered across the stonework. In the middle of the bridge there was a tower with an arch in its center through which they rode. Richard was not all that impressed having seen much more impressive structures in London.

As soon as the coach was off the bridge, the driver yelled *whoa!* to the horses, and the carriage came to a swaying stop.

"That's it," said the sheriff as he opened the door and stepped out.

Richard climbed out shakily. They had stopped in front of a public inn.

"Old Swan Inn," said the sheriff pointing up to a sign on the door that displayed a large white swan swimming in a dark pond. "Not a better place for board and room in the whole town. Well, good day to you," he said as he turned and walked toward the inn's door.

"Excuse me, sir," said Richard, still feeling a little unsteady on his feet. "Would you happen to know where John White lives?"

"Do I know him? Of course I know him. He works for me! Now," he said as he wiped his hands down the front of his coat and took a deep breath. Then he pointed with an outstretched hand. "Just go right up High Street here—let's see, one, two, three—to the third street. On your left is Silver Street. On the northwest corner of High and Silver streets is the jail. John White lives just west of the jail. Can't miss it."

Richard grabbed his bag from the boot of the coach and headed up the street. Bedford seemed like such a strange place compared to London. The dirt streets were wide and open. Behind the rows of houses which fronted on the streets there were fields or orchards right in the middle of town.

He walked along, past another large church on the left, and passed two small boys chasing a hoop with sticks.

At the third street—Silver Street—he noticed what had to be the jail. It was a two-story stone building with three narrow windows, each covered with an iron grill.

Richard did not recognize the man who answered the door in the house west of the jail. He was not much taller than Richard, round in the middle, and balding. What hair he still had was black and pulled back where it was tied at the back of his head in a limp ponytail. His clothes were rust colored and typical of most merchants—no excessive lace and frills. But one thing was unusual. Though his britches stopped at the knees, and stockings extended below them, he did not wear the common shoes of the day.

Instead, he had on a pair of boots, like a farmer or dock worker.

"I'm looking for John White," said Richard, feeling much better after his walk in the fresh air.

"You're looking at him," said the man in a rather brusque manner, his brow knitting together. "But if you've brought something for one of the prisoners, you'll either have to leave it with me or come back tomorrow about noon. I'm not running a public hostel here, so I don't have time to open the gate at everyone's beck and call."

"Uh—Uncle John?" Richard ventured, not certain whether this was his uncle or not.

"Uncle? Who are you, lad?" He squinted at Richard. "You can't be Eunice's boy, can you?"

"Yes, sir. I'm Richard Winslow."

"Well, well." The man's face smoothed into a smile. "Come in, my son. Come in! But what brings you all the way to Bedford? Where is your mother?" He looked up and down the street as though he expected to see some sort of carriage with the rest of the family in it.

John White pulled Richard through the door and called excitedly to his wife. "Agnes! Agnes! Come see who is here. You will never guess."

Agnes White came bustling in, middle-aged, round-cheeked, wiping her hands on her apron. "Richard," she cried, recognizing him immediately. "My, how you've grown. The last time we saw you, you were only half as high." She threw her arms open wide and embraced him in a warm hug.

"Where's my sister? Where's Eunice and the babies?" she bubbled.

Richard snickered inside. He wished his sisters were there to hear themselves called "babies."

Soon the three of them were sitting around the kitchen table with mugs of tea as Richard told his story.

John and Agnes White had no children, and because they were simple working people, they did not have any servants. But their snug cottage was warm and welcoming all the same.

As Richard finished his tale with what he'd seen at Westminster Abbey, Uncle John shook his head and frowned. "I don't know what this country is coming to," he said. "My jail is full and overflowing these days. And it's not with criminals, mind you—at least not what *I* would call criminals. Most of these are good, Christian people who just happen to be on the wrong side of the king. Though I don't think some of them even oppose him."

"You're the jail keeper?" asked Richard in surprise. Then he remembered what the sheriff had said about his Uncle John working for him.

"Oh yes," said Uncle John proudly. "We've been here about three years now. My back just couldn't take working the flour mill anymore. Too much lifting, ya know. Now I'm a *king's* man!" Then, realizing what he had said, he added quickly, "But that doesn't mean I have anything against your good father. I'm sure he's done nothing wrong, and that'll all come to light soon enough."

Finally, Richard asked the main question on his mind. "Uncle John, would it be all right if I stayed with you and Aunt Agnes for a while?"

Uncle John grinned. "Well, that all depends. I've been looking for a strong lad who can help me around the jail. You think you are up to such work? There's hauling hay and water and dumping the prisoners' waste buckets over in Saffron Ditch. It's not a pleasant task. You got a strong stomach?"

Richard remembered how he had almost lost his lunch riding in the coach that afternoon. The thought of having to empty waste buckets brought on another wave of nausea. But he took a deep breath and said, "I'm up to it."

"Good," said Uncle John as he clapped Richard on the shoulder. "A jailor you shall be!"

"Now, John," murmured Aunt Agnes. "He's just a lad. You mustn't work him too hard." She turned to her nephew and beamed. "Of course, you can stay with us for as long as you like—and if he works you too hard, you just let me know."

"Don't you go buttin' in, Agnes," growled Uncle John. "It'll do the lad good. He's nearly grown up, and a little hard work will make a man of him."

That night, after a simple meal of barley soup and hard, black bread, Richard had the best sleep he had had since his father was taken away. The little upstairs room under the thatch roof had a small window that looked out over the town of Bedford. A silver moon illuminated the shops, cottages, fields, and churches, making it seem as peaceful as the ripples on a pond—nothing like the hubbub that always filled a London night.

But the next morning, Richard got his introduction to the county jail of Bedfordshire. It had two floors above an underground dungeon. His Uncle John lifted the bar from the massive oak door, unlocked the iron bolt, and pulled it free with a clank. The door swung open, and he led Richard within.

"Here on the ground floor," said Uncle John, "is where we keep your average criminal—those waiting for trial or already sentenced to prison. There are two open rooms surrounded by several sleeping cells. As you can see, we are greatly overcrowded. It used to be nearly empty, just a thief now and then, especially around the time of the county fair. But now we've got close to fifty people in here, mostly religious nonconformists—Puritans, Baptists, Quakers, and a couple Presbyterians. I don't see any good reason for putting most of them in jail, myself, but then I don't make the laws."

They went through another heavy door and climbed the stairs to the second floor.

"I've had to put some of the nonconformists up here, but usually this floor is reserved for debtors."

On the second floor there was one common room and four sleeping rooms, much larger than those downstairs. Also, instead of the windows being narrow slits with iron grates over them, the windows on this floor were larger and covered only by bars.

When they came downstairs, Richard's uncle lit a

torch and opened another door. This one was bolted as securely as the front door had been. They went down eleven steps into the dungeon.

"Is there anyone down here?" asked Richard nervously, looking around the dingy place.

"That there is, in both cells," said Uncle John. "In there" —he pointed to a heavy door with no window in it— "we have John Fox. He's raging mad and accused of murder. We feed him through that slit under the door. He'll probably hang."

"How 'bout in there?" Richard pointed to the other door. It had a small window in it with an iron grate over it.

"You can look in there. That cell has one small window up at ground level. We keep a woman named Elizabeth Pratt in there. They say she's a witch, but I can't believe she ever did anything so bad."

Richard looked through the small hole in the door that was covered with an iron grate. In the far corner, in the dim light from a tiny slit window near the ceiling, he could make out a lump under a blanket on a pile of straw.

"Now, she ain't dangerous," said Uncle John, "not unless you are afraid of her casting a spell over you. So every few days you'll be replacing her straw and doing what you can for her. I wouldn't keep her in there, except the court requires me to. It's a terrible thing."

"Why do you do it then?" asked Richard.

John White shrugged. "I don't make the law. It's just my duty to uphold it."

Richard frowned. "But why carry out an unjust law?"

"Ah-ha! You're thinking of your father being thrown into the Tower. Why didn't some good-hearted guard turn his head the other way and let him flee? But what good would it have done? That would have made a fugitive of your father . . . and a criminal of the guard. I don't doubt that your father's an honorable man, and I've known the law to be unfair more than once. But—" John White paused and looked back up the dark dungeon steps. He stood there staring as though he could see through the stone walls of the jail to some scene miles away. Suddenly, he shook his head and brusquely continued, "It is a terrible thing to land in prison. Workin' here you'll see that for yourself, and you'll want to stay out . . . by obeying the law, even the parts you *don't* like."

Chapter 4

The Parolee

THE VERY NEXT DAY Richard began his job carrying food and straw to the prisoners and emptying the stinking waste buckets. It was hard work, and at first he resented it. Criminals, after all, were lowlife sorts, a class of people far below himself. He avoided their eyes, did his job as quickly as he could, and got out of there. But one day as he brought back the empty waste buckets, he had a startling thought: his father hadn't landed in prison for being a lowlife.

These were real people in this jail; some of them like his father.

He began to take more notice of the prisoners.

Theirs was a hard life, made harder by the crowded conditions. There was no means of taking a bath in the jail and no fireplaces or brazier pans holding burning coals for warmth. This made life easier for Richard since he didn't have to haul coal or firewood. But he couldn't imagine how the inmates warmed themselves in the winter.

"They don't," his uncle said when Richard asked. "Sometimes prisoners get what's called jail fever, and since we don't have an infirmary, some of them die. It's too bad, but with no heat, the place never really dries out."

Each prisoner received a quarter of a loaf of bread per day, and for that the prisoner had to pay. Any other food had to be brought in from the outside by family and friends.

After working in the jail awhile, Richard began to recognize the family members who stopped by regularly to visit their imprisoned loved ones. He tried not to think about his father alone with no visitors in the Tower. There was nothing he could do about it yet. Soon, though, he would have to think of a way to return to London and attempt a visit. What if his father had nothing more than bread and water to eat? What if he needed someone to bring him better food like these prisoners got from their families?

One of the regular visitors at the Bedfordshire jail was a girl about Richard's own age who came each day at noon with a widemouthed jug of soup for one of the prisoners. His uncle let her into the jail with a friendly welcome, calling her Mary.

She was an attractive girl with thick, dark hair and clear skin the color of cream. Richard was watching her intently one day, trying to figure why she walked in a slightly stiff manner and never spoke to him. *Maybe she's too embarrassed,* he concluded. He knew that feeling, not wanting other people to know that his father was in prison.

Seeing him watching her, his uncle said, "Interesting girl, that Mary Bunyan. She lives a block up Mill Lane on the corner of Cuthbert Street. More dependable than a sundial. A sundial requires the sun to be out, but she's here *every day*—by noon—sunshine or rain. You'd never know she's blind."

"What?" exclaimed Richard. "She can't see?"

"Not a bit, but it doesn't stop her. She goes all over town."

Astonished, Richard watched the girl as she moved across the crowded common room to the far side where a man sat on a bench working intently with his hands. She moved in that slow, stiff manner he had previously noticed, looking straight ahead. And then he saw it. She was feeling her way with her feet, and when her toe touched the leg of a man sleeping in the middle of the floor, she easily turned to the side without losing her balance.

It was amazing! Richard remembered times when as a younger boy he had pretended to be blind, trying to walk around and do things with his eyes closed just to see what it was like. His game had never lasted more than a few minutes before he squinted one eye open and peeked. It was just too hard.

But this girl seemed to manage with only the slightest stiffness.

The next day when she arrived, John White was away from the jail taking care of some business. "Hello, Mary," Richard said boldly as he let her in.

"Good day," the girl said tentatively. "I don't think I know you. You sound young. Are you a—?"

"No, I'm not a prisoner. I work here, helping my uncle. I'm Richard Winslow . . . from London," he added as an afterthought.

"Oh."

"I've seen you bringing soup every day. Is that tinker your father?" Richard pointed to the man who spent his days working over a small bench. His uncle had told him that the man was a tinker, but of course, he couldn't repair pots and pans or make knives in jail. So he had found some small craft with which to make money.

"Yes." She started to move on into the common room.

"What's his name?" asked Richard, eager to learn more about this remarkable girl who could walk all around town even though she was blind.

"His name is John Bunyan, and he doesn't belong here."

"Well, why is he here then?" Richard said in a rather challenging tone of voice.

"He was preaching without a license." She took another step, then turned back and said, "Why don't you come and meet him? He can tell you all about it."

Richard tentatively followed the girl into the common room and over to the bench where her father sat and worked. The man was average height, in his early thirties, his shoulder-length light brown hair hiding his face as he bent over his task. It was the first time Richard had paid any attention to what the tinker was doing, but he quickly saw that the man was making laces for women's corsets. He had piles of them bundled together. He cut them to length and crimped brass tags on each end to keep them from unraveling.

"Mary!" said the prisoner with warm joy in his voice, lifting his face. It was a broad, open face, with wide-set brown eyes and a strong nose. One eyebrow arched slightly higher than the other. "It's so good to see you. Here, let me take that jug. Hmmm, it smells so good." John Bunyan took a sip. "Thank you, Mary. Here, sit down." He moved his things off the bench, and the girl sat beside him.

Richard stood by awkwardly during this family greeting. Finally, Mary said, "Father, this is Richard Winslow. He wants to know why you are in prison."

"Oh, he does, does he? Why, for preaching God's Word, lad," said Bunyan, looking up at the lanky boy standing near him.

"What's wrong with preaching?"

The man grinned ruefully. "That's what I'd like to know. The Bible plainly says, 'Preach the word,' and that's all I was doing. But, now that the king has returned and the state church is back in power, we nonconformists aren't tolerated. One would think that some of the freedoms gained under Cromwell would last. But I guess he made too many enemies. So, since I didn't have a license, they said I couldn't preach."

Mary added, "Father could get released today if he would promise to not preach anymore, but he won't."

Richard frowned. The girl spoke with pride rather than resentment in her voice. It confused Richard. "Why not promise, Mr. Bunyan?"

"How can I promise to *not* do something my Lord has commanded me to do?"

"Well . . ." Richard fumbled for an answer. "For the sake of your family, obviously! My father is in prison, too, and I know what grief it brings," he blurted out.

"Is he, now?" said John Bunyan with a broad smile. "And why might he be held?"

Richard froze. He had not intended to tell anyone other than his aunt and uncle about his father's imprisonment. Personal information in the hands of the wrong people could be dangerous, and he did not really know whether this John Bunyan was trustworthy or not. "It was nothing," said Richard stiffly, "just some political confusion that will soon be straightened out."

Bunyan's eyebrows went up. "Yes," he said, "political confusion can be nearly as bad as religious confusion."

Richard withdrew and went back to his work of distributing new straw to the sleeping cells. Later, when Mary was ready to go home, he let her out but did not speak to her.

✧ ✧ ✧ ✧

The next day was Sunday, and Richard went early to carry a bucket of water around to the prisoners. Suddenly, he was surprised to see his uncle come into the jail and release John Bunyan.

Richard hurried to his uncle's side. "Is he free?"

"Oh no. He just wanted to go to church this morning—some special meeting or something."

"But aren't you afraid that he will escape?"

"Bunyan? Not in the least. He could get out of jail any day if he would just promise not to preach, but he won't make such a promise. Says he has to obey God rather than man." John White shrugged. "Since he's in jail by his own choice, I have no reason to think he will flee the county. Besides, as I told you the other day, his wife and family just live over on Cuthbert Street. So where would he go?"

Richard returned to his chores, feeling confused and unsettled. *So it's true,* he thought. *This man Bunyan could be released any time simply by promising not to preach anymore.* The information nagged at Richard's thoughts. *Why would a man abandon his family and choose to rot in jail if he could get out simply by making a promise to not preach?* The more he thought about it, the more upset he became, until he realized that he was outright angry at the man.

John Bunyan returned to jail that afternoon, just as Richard's uncle had said he would, and with him came his daughter Mary. Richard admitted them both into the jail, then followed them into the sleeping room Bunyan shared with three other men who were out in the common room at the time gambling with homemade dice carved from bones.

Richard had to say something—for the sake of Bunyan's blind daughter, he told himself. "As I told you yesterday," he blurted, challenging, "my father is in prison, too. If I knew he could get out simply by making a promise, I'd be very upset if he refused to do so." He looked at Mary, who was staring in his direction, but with her unseeing eyes, she did not focus on his face. "You can't imagine how hard it is on my poor mother for him to be in prison." In spite of himself, Richard's voice quavered.

"So you think I should make the promise?" said Bunyan.

Richard shrugged, but it was a shrug that said absolutely yes.

John Bunyan squinted, and Richard saw tears gather in the man's eyes. "I've thought very hard about that myself," he said, "but maybe I can explain myself by telling you a story. Mary, would you like a story?"

"Oh yes, Father." The girl's face lit up. "You tell such good stories."

"Both of you—sit down here on the straw, and I'll see what I can do."

A story? What kind of answer was this? Richard hesitated a moment, knowing fleas and lice infested the prison, especially the straw bedding. But he handled it every day, and he was curious so he sat down.

"Once upon a time," began John Bunyan, "there was a man—we'll call him Pilgrim.

Pilgrim had a tremendous pack on his back that he could not take off. But he also had a book in his hand. He opened the book hoping for some instructions for how to remove his burden. But as he read, he began to cry and tremble.

Soon he let out a great moan and said, "What shall I do?"

In this sad state, he went home and tried—as long as he could—to keep his feelings from his wife and children. But he could not keep silent for long. Finally, he said, "My dear wife, and you my own dear children, I'm very upset because of this burden I'm carrying on my back. It is made of sin, and I must find a way to become free of it."

His family looked at the pack on his back and shrugged. Everyone in the city carried some sort of a burden, and no one had ever thought of taking it off, so why should Pilgrim?

Then he said, "I have also learned that this city of ours shall be destroyed with fire from heaven for all its sin. If we cannot find some way to escape, we shall all be destroyed."

The more Pilgrim talked, the more his family frowned. They did not believe what he was saying, and so they became more and more

concerned that he might be going crazy.

As it drew toward night, they whispered to one another the hope that sleep might settle his brain. "Come, Dear," said the woman, "it's time for bed. Have a cup of warm milk and get some sleep. Tomorrow you will feel better."

But the night was as troublesome to Pilgrim as the day. Instead of sleeping, he spent it in sighs and tears. In the morning his children said, "How are you feeling now, Papa?"

"Worse and worse," he said. "We must all leave this place and find a way to get these burdens off our backs."

But the more he talked, the more they resisted. Finally, they tried to drive away what they thought was craziness by scolding him to straighten up. When that didn't work, they tried begging him to come around.

Finally, the wife said, "Let's just leave him alone, and maybe he'll come to his senses on his own." So they left his bedroom and carried on their life as normally as possible.

Pilgrim took the opportunity to pray for them and read his book, for the book he had was the Bible. It was, in fact, from the Bible that he had learned that the burden on his back was sin and that the sin of the whole city would lead to destruction.

The standoff continued for several days. Sometimes Pilgrim prayed and read in his room, and sometimes he went for walks in the fields outside the city. When he was by himself, he would cry out loud, "What shall I do to be saved?"

One day when Pilgrim was walking in the field praying, a man approached and said, "Hello. My name is Evangelist. You seem upset. Why are you crying?"

Pilgrim answered, "Sir, in reading this book, I discovered that I am going to die and after that I must face judgment. I'm afraid to die and even more afraid to face the judgment."

Evangelist rubbed his chin. "Why are you so afraid to die? Isn't this world full enough of troubles that you'd be glad to get out of it?"

"Oh, no," said Pilgrim. "This burden upon my back would sink me lower than the grave, and I would slip into hell. I don't think I could take that. Why, I wouldn't last a day in prison. So how could I stand hell? It's the thoughts of these things that make me cry."

Then Evangelist said, "If this is your condition, why are you standing still?"

"Where should I go?" asked Pilgrim.

At that, Evangelist handed Pilgrim a parchment scroll with the words, "Flee from the wrath to come!" written on it.

"But to where?" cried Pilgrim in great confusion.

Evangelist pointed across the plain and said, "Do you see that gate almost to the horizon?"

"Can't say as I do," answered Pilgrim.

"Well, can you see that light in the sky—like a star?"

"Yes."

"Go directly toward it," continued Evangelist. "And when you get across the plain, you'll come to the gate. Knock at it, and you will be told what to do."

So Pilgrim began to run. But he had not gone far when his wife and children, seeing what he was doing, began to call after him begging him to return. But Pilgrim put his fingers in his ears and ran on, crying, "Life! Life! Eternal life!" And he would not look back but fled across the plain.

John Bunyan stopped talking and leaned back against the wall of his cell, crossing his arms on his chest. The story was obviously over.

"But, Father," cried Mary, "did Pilgrim get rid of his burden? What happened to him?"

Chapter 5

Into Enemy Territory

JOHN BUNYAN SMILED at his daughter's questions. "I guess you'll have to wait for some other time to find out what happened to poor Pilgrim," he said as he reached out and patted Mary's hand. "I was trying to tell a story to answer Richard's question. Does that help you understand, son?"

Richard furrowed his brow as he thought about the story of Pilgrim leaving his home and family. It was such a mysterious story, as though the prisoner had been telling a riddle. He felt there was more meaning in it than he realized. But as far as the man leaving home . . . "I guess," he ventured, "if Pilgrim knew something that no one else would believe— not even his family—he

would have to act on that knowledge."

"Very good," said John Bunyan. "The story is an allegory, a pretend story that symbolizes spiritual truths. And you figured out the exact point I was trying to make. Now, my wife and children have not 'cried after' me like poor Pilgrim's family did. They have been completely supportive. As you can see, Mary brings me food every day, and my dear wife, Elizabeth, comes with the other children to visit as often as she can. But with or without their support, I would have to obey God's call just as Pilgrim did."

"Seems kind of disloyal to me," Richard muttered. "They need you!"

John Bunyan was silent for several moments, and again Richard saw tears come to his eyes as he looked at his blind daughter. Finally, in a husky voice he said, "Yes, they do need me. Some men leave their families for their own selfish reasons, but for me, there is no greater sacrifice. I take no pleasure in my condition. But what do you think Jesus meant when He said, 'He that loveth father or mother . . . son or daughter more than me is not worthy of me'?"

"I'm . . . not sure," Richard admitted.

"I think He meant that there are times when we all must choose between what other people want us to do and what God wants to do. Whenever we face one of those choices, we must obey God rather than other people, even our own families. That's why I'm in this jail, you know. In my case it wasn't my family who opposed my call, it was the king."

Richard got up. He was feeling awkward with

what John Bunyan was saying, but he didn't know why. "Thank you for the story," he said lamely and walked out of the tinker's cell. Aunt Agnes would want him home for tea, anyway.

Richard did not talk to John Bunyan for the next few days, and when next he did, it was at Bunyan's request.

"Take a break, lad," the tinker said as Richard raked up the old straw. "I have something to ask you." They were in the common room, and Bunyan was again working at his bench cutting and tagging laces. By selling them for a few pennies per hundred, he earned enough for food for himself and his family. Richard had learned that Elizabeth Bunyan also took in laundry and mending to help ends meet.

"Here, lad, sit down," said Bunyan. "I've been wanting to ask you about your father. Would you mind telling me why he is in prison?"

Richard looked around at the other prisoners. Several were within earshot. "Out in the exercise yard," he said. There was a small, walled courtyard that the prisoners were allowed to walk around in when Richard or his uncle had the time to guard them.

Security in the Bedford jail was not as tight as it might have been in a large city prison. The chances of escape were slim. Most prisoners had no place where they could run to evade the law. In the En-

glish countryside, everyone was attached to some landowner either directly as a servant or as a tenant renting a farm from the landlord. Even the landowners considered the king their "lord." In one way or another, everyone had a master, someone to whom he was accountable. Any "masterless" men roaming the English countryside were suspect and could be immediately arrested by a local lord. In towns, things were a little different. There were craftsmen and shop owners and other merchants who weren't directly responsible to an overlord. But they belonged to the town where everyone knew them and could vouch for them.

Because fleeing was so difficult, it was easier to keep someone in jail than it might seem. Nonetheless, the wall around the small courtyard was tall and impossible to climb over while a jailer was on duty.

As Richard and John Bunyan walked in the exercise yard, Richard related how his father had been arrested in the middle of the night because of his association with Oliver Cromwell. Then he told how he'd seen Cromwell's body taken from its tomb and hung near Westminster Abbey, and how his mother had concluded it was too dangerous to remain in London.

"So that's why I came here," said Richard. "My mother and sisters went to Scotland by ship. It's been almost a month. As soon as I get a chance, I'm going back to London to visit my father and see if there is some way I can help."

"If your father worked closely with Oliver Cromwell," asked Bunyan, "was he a Puritan?"

Richard shrugged. He had heard the term used often, but he didn't know exactly what a Puritan was.

"Well, I am a Baptist myself, but Puritans are not all that different," said John Bunyan. "They want to get back to the *pure* Gospel, you might say. The Church of England has gotten so caught up in politics and ritual that the souls of the common people have been neglected. But it is not just the common people. The king and many of the lords and nobles live such wicked lives that they provide no fit example."

Bunyan laid a hand on Richard's shoulder as they walked. "The Bible says, 'All have sinned,' but the state church does not guide the people to conversion. How can one become acceptable to God? How can one live a pure and holy life? These are the central questions of a true and pure religion."

Richard nodded thoughtfully. "Yes, my mother often said the same things. My father took us all to church services every Sunday—it was the thing to do, I guess—but at home, it was my mother who read the Scriptures to us and prayed with us each night. My father thought that was taking religion a bit too far—but that doesn't mean he deserves to be in prison," he added quickly.

"No. I'm sure he doesn't," agreed John Bunyan. The two walked in silence for several moments, then Bunyan said, "I am planning on going to London next week. Do you want me to ask around about your father?"

"What? London?" Richard said in shock. "I know Uncle John allowed you to go to church for a few hours last Sunday, but—London? You'd be gone for several days! He would never allow that."

Bunyan pursed his lips. "I'll allow that you might be right, but then again, I think he will trust me with the trip. He knows I'll return. There's no question about that."

"If he does let you go," said Richard, hardly daring to trust the eagerness he felt, "I would be most grateful if you would check on my father." He stopped with a worried look on his face as he remembered. "However, our butler didn't think anyone but family could get in to see him. But maybe, maybe" —he was thinking fast— "maybe I could go with you. If I were to go along, Uncle John would be more likely to let you go, wouldn't he? And when we got there, I could try to visit my father. What do you say about that?"

"Hmmm, I don't think having his nephew along would make much difference for your uncle. Either he'll let me go on my good word or not." Bunyan stopped walking and looked Richard in the eye, being only slightly taller than the boy. "You might have a chance to see your father. But what if someone traces you back to me or the underground church in London? It's not safe these days to be connected to someone in prison."

"What underground church? I don't know of any underground church in London or anywhere else."

"Ah, of course not. Excuse me for mentioning it. Furthermore, it's best you don't know anything about it, either, so don't ask any more questions."

To Richard's amazement, his uncle not only agreed to John Bunyan's trip but allowed him to accompanying the tinker. He even said, "Richard, you're becoming a man. I'll make you my unofficial deputy to see that this man returns as promised."

His going *had* made a difference. Richard looked over at John Bunyan with a smug grin on his face. Bunyan shrugged and smiled back, and then Richard began to wonder whether his uncle was just humoring him, trying to make him *feel* grown-up. Oh well, it didn't make any difference; at least he was going to visit his father.

They caught a ride on the weekly postal coach on Tuesday afternoon. This time, the trip over the rough country road from Bedford to the Great North Road did not make Richard sick. Maybe the road was a little smoother, or maybe he had his mind on other things. In any case, the two-day trip went by quickly, and he and John Bunyan arrived in London tired but eager.

In London, Bunyan took Richard to a house in a part of the city that Richard had never visited. "Elder Barnabas," Bunyan said once they had stepped inside, "I'd like you to meet—" He paused as though he were uncertain what to call Richard. "Yes, well,

I'd like you to meet Brother Richard."

Richard shook the older man's hand, and they were led into a small sitting room crowded already with about thirty people. Everyone was introduced simply as Brother or Sister, with no last names. Food was brought in for the two visitors from out of town, and Richard suddenly realized that they had been expected. The whole group had gathered because John Bunyan was visiting. It had to be the secret church Bunyan had mentioned.

Soon someone started the group singing hymns, and then, when John Bunyan had finished eating, Elder Barnabas stood up. "O Lord," he prayed, "we thank Thee for sustaining our Brother John, and we ask your blessing on him now as he brings us Thy word. Amen."

The room was warm, and Bunyan had only begun to speak when Richard's head began to nod. Embarrassed, he jerked awake and tried to listen. But he was so tired from the trip that he couldn't pay attention.

Finally, a woman touched him on the shoulder and whispered, "Would you like to go to bed? It's all right."

Chapter 6

The Tower of London

THE ROOM TO WHICH RICHARD WAS SHOWN was small with two hard cots in it. As he sat down on one of them, he couldn't help think that this would probably be the best bed John Bunyan had slept on for months.

But surprisingly, as soon as Richard lay down to sleep, he felt wide awake. In the morning, he would go to the Tower and try to see his father. But what if the guards wouldn't let him in? What if someone wanted to capture the rest of the family? What if his father was sick? What if he had already been condemned to death?

The questions were too many and too big to cope with, and they swirled around inside his mind, chasing away every hint of sleepiness.

In about an hour, John Bunyan came into the room carrying a small candle and noticed Richard's eyes open. "I thought you'd be in dreamland long before now. What's the problem?"

Richard shrugged and sat up, swinging his feet to the floor.

"Thinking about tomorrow?"

"Yes, I guess so. I—I just don't know what's going to happen. What if they arrest me?"

John Bunyan looked at Richard for a few minutes, then sat down on the cot across from him, setting the candle on a bedside table. "You remember that story I told you and Mary?"

"Yes, the one about Pilgrim?"

"Exactly. Let me tell you another story about Pilgrim." John Bunyan sat back on his cot so that the wall became a support for his back. He pursed his lips and looked up toward the ceiling as though the story were written there in the dark for him to read. Then he began.

After many difficulties and delays, Pilgrim succeeded in crossing the plain to find the gate that Evangelist had described. The gate opened onto the long, narrow road leading to the Heavenly City. And at the gate, as Evangelist had promised, Pilgrim received instructions for continuing his journey.

Not far beyond the gate, he went up a small rise to where a cross stood. Long ago on that cross, a Man had taken the punishment

Pilgrim deserved for all his sins. As Pilgrim gratefully knelt at the base of the cross, his burden fell from his back and rolled down the hill.

Pilgrim leaped up in joy, tears streaming down his face. Then he saw three shining beings. The first said, "Your sins are forgiven." The second took his rags and gave him new clothing. The third gave him a scroll to present at the gate of the Heavenly City.

Even though his burden of sin was gone, Pilgrim's journey was not over, because he had determined to travel on to the Heavenly City where he would find safety and peace. So on he went through many hardships and trials. He met various companions on his trip. Some were faithful and true and helped him on his way. Others led him astray or discouraged him.

One day as Pilgrim was climbing a particularly steep mountain, he stopped to rest under a pleasant tree. It had been planted there by the Lord of the mountain to refresh weary travelers like Pilgrim.

While he was resting, he pulled his Bible out of his pocket and read to comfort himself with the promises he found within. At last, he fell asleep, and his Bible slipped out of his hand.

When he awoke a short time later, the words of the last verse he had read were fresh in his mind: "Go to the ant, thou sluggard; consider her ways and be wise." Immediately, Pilgrim jumped to his feet and hurried on his way so as to not waste the precious hours of daylight that remained.

When he got up to the top of the mountain, there came two men running to meet him. The first introduced himself breathlessly as Timid, and the second said, "And I am Mistrust."

"But, sirs," said Pilgrim, "what's the matter? You run the wrong way."

"Oh," moaned Timid, "we were going to the Heavenly City and had gotten past so many difficult places, but the farther we go, the more danger we meet with. So, we turned around and are going back again."

"Yes," said Mistrust with wide eyes of fear, "not far ahead of you lie a couple of lions in the way. We couldn't tell whether they were asleep or awake, but we knew that if we came within reach of them, they would pull us to pieces."

"This is frightful," said Pilgrim. "But where can anyone run to be safe? If I go back with you to my old town—a town that I now call the City of Destruction—that's exactly what will happen to me. I will certainly be destroyed. But if I go forward and succeed in reaching the Heavenly City, I will be safe. But you say the path gets harder. So what am I to do?"

Pilgrim tested his choices, describing them again: "To go back is nothing but death. To go forward involves the *fear* of death, but if I make it, there is life everlasting beyond it." Pilgrim clapped his hands and declared, "I will go forward!"

No sooner had he made his choice than Mistrust and Timid ran down the hill heading back to the old country. Thinking again of the warning they had given him, Pilgrim felt in his pocket for his Bible so that he could read a few words of encouragement.

It was not there! In deep distress, Pilgrim felt around. Could he have put it someplace else? But no. It was missing. This was serious. He had wanted simply to read a few words of comfort, but not having the book was far more serious. For it told him how to get to the Heavenly City. He had to have it!

Finally, he calmed himself enough to recall the last time he had it, and then he remembered his nap under the tree. "I must have left it there," he moaned. What carelessness. There was nothing to do but go back for it. So back he started, resenting the time he wasted in retracing his steps.

When he got to the tree and saw his little Bible lying there on the ground, he had mixed feelings. "One should never sleep in the midst of difficulty!" he scolded himself. "Look at all the time I have wasted." But he was also very joyful at having found his little Bible. He snatched it up and stuffed it in his pocket securely so as never to lose it again. "Thank You, God," he murmured, "for directing my eyes to the place where I found it."

Then he turned around again and scurried back up the hill. But before he got to the top, the sun went down, and he was again reminded of his foolishness for sleeping during the day. "Now my pathway is dark, and there are all sorts of noises out there that I won't be able to identify."

He remembered the story that Mistrust and Timid told him about the fearful lions. Pilgrim said to himself, "These beasts roam in the night for their prey, and if I meet them in the dark, what will I do? How will I escape being torn in pieces?"

But he did not turn back, and in a short time, he looked up and saw not far ahead a beautiful inn that stood beside his path. "Ah," he sighed, "if only I can reach that inn, then I will gain a safe night's rest." So on he slogged.

But before he had gone far, he entered a narrow canyon. Suddenly, he spied two lions. *Now*, thought he, *now I see the dangers that caused Mistrust and Timid to turn back. Maybe I should go back, too.* Fear caused him to tremble. It seemed that nothing but death lay before him.

Just then the porter came out of the inn and put his hands to his mouth. "Good traveler," he called, "do not fear the lions, for they are chained, and are placed there to test the faith of those who come this way. Those who have no faith always turn back, but if you will keep in the middle of the path, no harm will come to you."

Then, trembling for fear of the lions, Pilgrim followed the directions of the porter and moved on through the canyon. The lions roared and leaped at the ends of their chains. But their tethers held fast, and he proceeded unharmed.

His heart was beating wildly once he had reached safety at the end of the canyon, but he clapped his hands joyfully and went on up to the gate of the inn.

"Good sir," said Pilgrim to the porter, "is there room for me to spend the night here?"

"That there is, my young friend," said the porter as he opened the gate wide. "The Lord of the mountain built this house for the very likes of you. Come in, and take your rest."

While John Bunyan was telling the story, Richard had lain back down on his cot, and as the storyteller concluded with the phrase, ". . . and take your rest," Richard's eyes closed and he fell asleep.

During the night Richard woke up, uncertain where he was. Then he heard the London night sounds and remembered the journey . . . and John Bunyan's story about Pilgrim.

As he stared into the darkness, he thought, *I'm like Pilgrim, away from my family . . . on a journey with dangers and uncertainty ahead . . . but am I still carrying that pack of sins on my back?* As he thought about the story, he remembered kneeling at his mother's knee as a child, asking Jesus to forgive his sins. He felt a leap of recognition. Hearing Pilgrim's story, he understood more what his mother had been teaching him and his sisters.

Richard turned his head toward the cot where his companion slept. He wanted to tell John Bunyan that he, too, was a believer . . . but the man was snoring softly.

The next day, with the fantastic images of Pilgrim's journey still floating in his mind, Richard headed for the Tower of London. On the way through London's narrow streets, he imagined himself passing through the canyon where Pilgrim approached the inn. Of course, he was not headed to a pleasant inn for some rest and relaxation, but the temptation to turn back out of timidity and mistrust were just as real.

Suddenly, to his utter amazement, Richard noticed a huge stone building—some government build-

ing or something—with two enormous lions sitting
on either side of the columned entrance. He had to

look twice to reassure himself that they were only stone. The sight was awesome. They had been carved to look frightening, but Richard took courage in seeing them. The Lord would be with him just like He had been with Pilgrim. All he needed was a little faith.

Did John Bunyan know what streets I would be walking down on my way to the Tower? Richard wondered. *Did he remember those lions and build his story around them just for my sake?*

The guard at the gate to the Tower was nowhere near as welcoming as the porter of the beautiful inn where Pilgrim stayed. But after asking a dozen questions, he did swing the creaking gate open and allowed Richard to enter.

"Wait here," he commanded, pointing to a small alcove in the prison's wall.

Richard waited and waited and waited. Finally, another guard arrived and said, "Are you here to see Obadiah Winslow?"

"Yes, sir," said Richard in a pleasant voice. The man looked like he had had all the unpleasantness he could stand for one day, and Richard knew that he needed his good will.

They passed through locked door after locked door and down long, stone passages and up many stairs. By the time the man stopped before a cell and fumbled for his keys, Richard had no idea where he was.

"You have twenty minutes," the guard barked and swung open the heavy door.

For a few seconds, Richard just stood in the doorway, trying to adjust his eyes to the dim light.

"Richard!" said his father's familiar voice, taking three steps across the small cell and embracing his son. "It's so good to see you!"

Richard hugged his father for a long time. His father felt much thinner, but his embrace was strong, and his voice sounded firm. When his father finally held him at arm's length, Richard noticed that his father had grown a short beard. He had never seen his father with a beard, and this one was not trimmed but just rough whiskers. There was gray in it, too, something Richard had never noticed in his father's hair before.

Richard started to pepper his father with questions about how he was doing, but Mr. Winslow dismissed his questions by saying, "Oh, I'm doing all right. They feed me and bring me things to read, but I can't seem to get any writing material. I guess I fall between the cracks." He gave a short laugh. "I was too important to ignore but not important enough to get any special treatment."

Richard looked around. The cell was about six feet wide and ten feet long. High on one end was a small slit window. There was a sleeping mat on the floor and a table, chair, and candle. Briefly Richard wondered whether it was better to be crowded into a common jail like the one in Bedford or to have a cell all to one's self—with the obvious loneliness of being alone.

"Tell me about yourself, and your mother and the

girls," his father insisted.

Richard told him about his mother and sisters going to Scotland the day after his arrest, while his father nodded approval and asked a few questions. Then Richard told about his being in Bedford, living with Uncle John and Aunt Agnes. He did not say that he was working in a jail.

"But what's happening with your case, Father? Is there anything I can do?"

His father's shoulders fell in discouragement. "I don't know," he said. "Everything takes so long. I have not yet even spoken to a lawyer. I don't even know why they are holding me. It has something to do with my working for Oliver Cromwell."

Mr. Winslow got up and paced back and forth in his tiny space. Richard sensed that he had already put in many miles on that short path. Then his father slammed his fist into the palm of his hand. "If only Cromwell were still alive," he said. "He could prove that I don't belong here."

"What do you mean, Father?"

Just then the door of the cell swung open and the jailer barked, "Time's up! Come along, boy."

The guard grabbed Richard by the arm with an iron grip and pulled him toward the door.

"Wait!" protested Richard. "What were you saying, Father? What could Cromwell do?" He looked back over his shoulder as the guard pulled him out of the cell, and at the last moment saw his father shaking his head in caution with a worried frown on his face.

'Cromwell can rot in his grave, for all I care," his father called after him.

But as Richard walked through the dingy passages of the Tower, he was certain that was not what his father had meant to say.

Chapter 7

The Clampdown

THE DAY AFTER RICHARD and John Bunyan got back to Bedford, there came a loud knock at the jail door. Richard answered it and found a familiar-looking man in a powdered wig standing in the rain.

"Well, well, if it isn't my traveling companion," the man said as he shook the water off his broad-brimmed hat and stepped into the small entry room. "Have you recovered from that awful coach ride yet?"

"That I have, sir," said Richard, recognizing the sheriff of Bedfordshire who had ridden in the coach with him when he first came to Bedford. "I expect you'll be wanting to speak with my uncle. He's over at the house. But I was on my way there just now. Can I take you?"

"I'd be most pleased. I hear you are helping your uncle around the jail these days. Do you think you will make a life of it?"

Not likely, Richard thought as he opened the door, let the guest out, and locked the jail tightly behind himself.

A few minutes later, when all three were seated around the table in the White family's house drinking tea, Edmund Wylde turned to John White and said seriously, "John, I don't usually interfere with your running of the jail as long as everything goes smoothly. But recently some of the magistrates got wind of the liberties you're allowing John Bunyan, and they don't like it. I've been told to instruct you to keep him on the premises under lock and key. No more going to church or whatever you've been allowing."

John White pursed his lips and frowned, looking down into his teacup as though he were counting the leaves. "Excuse me for saying so, sir, but I hardly see why that's necessary. You and I both know that Bunyan's not going anywhere. His word's good as gold. Why, this past weekend I let him go to London, and he came back just as he promised."

"You . . . you *what*? You let him go all the way to London?" The sheriff looked like he might have a stroke. "Oh, John, this could mean big trouble."

"Why? He's in the jail right now, working on his tagged laces or writing one of his tracts. You can go see for yourself."

"That's not it, John. The magistrates think he may be part of those Fifth Monarchy men. And if they hear that he went off to London, they'll be sure he was talking with some secret group to conspire against the king."

John White snorted. "Edmund, I don't even know what this so-called Fifth Monarchy group is, but Bunyan's just a simple tinker. He was born over in Elstow. You even knew his parents. He's lived here for years. He's no conspirator. You know that as well as I do."

"All the same, John. We have no idea what he did in London. Who knows what he was doing there!"

"Well, Richard here knows. He went with him." John White smiled broadly at his nephew, then turned back to Edmund Wylde. "If any of those stuffy magistrates complain, you tell them that Bunyan didn't go to London alone. He went under guard. I sent my deputy with him."

Edmund looked over at Richard and scowled. "John, I don't mind you using the boy around the jail, but he's not a king's guard, and you have no authority to deputize him." His face had become red with emotion, and he was speaking louder, almost angrily, right into John White's face. "This is serious! Either you keep Bunyan in jail, or you are out of your position. Is that understood?"

John White shrugged and said, "Of course, you're the sheriff . . . but I still don't think any harm was done. He just went to some church meeting or something. You know Bunyan. If he's not preaching to a congregation somewhere, he'll gather up the mice in jail to hear him give a sermon."

Edmund Wylde sighed with relief and he leaned back more easily. "I suppose it wouldn't hurt if the mice got a little religion. Seems like they are always thievin' and robbin'." He laughed, easing the tension.

Then he leaned forward again and said, "So your nephew, here, went to London with him, did he?" Then he turned to Richard. "What happened while you were there, lad? Did he meet with any secret groups or anything?"

Richard swallowed hard. It felt like all the blood had drained out of his head, and for a moment he thought he was going to faint. He swallowed again, and finally his voice came out in a kind of squeak. "He just preached." It was all he could say.

" 'Preached'?" said the sheriff as though that were an unbelievable activity. There was silence as he waited for Richard to explain more.

But Richard was thinking about the meeting of the secret Puritan church. He remembered the singing and the warmth of the room after his long and tiring journey. John Bunyan had begun to speak when Richard had nodded off to sleep. The next thing he had known, a woman had tapped him on the shoulder and shown him up to his bed. And then it had been some time before Bunyan came up. He couldn't say for sure what had gone on at the meeting. *Could they have been conspirators?* he wondered.

But before he was required to answer, his uncle

came to his rescue. "Of course, he preached, Edmund. What else would Bunyan do? Isn't that what got him into this jail in the first place? He's a preacher, not a revolutionary. You know that. Now leave the boy alone."

"Yes, yes, John," said the sheriff, holding his hand out to calm John White, but he wasn't finished questioning Richard. "But was this a regular church like Saint Cuthbert's or Saint Paul's?"

"No. It was just in someone's house," admitted Richard. He didn't know what was happening. He had grown to like John Bunyan, and he didn't want to say anything that might get him into trouble.

"Does he ever talk about strange things around you, like he was speaking of some other country or something?" pressed the sheriff.

Richard remembered the Pilgrim stories. Yes, John Bunyan had spoken of strange things—of the very "lions" he had seen on the way to the Tower—but did that make him an enemy of the king? No. He couldn't believe it. Finally, Richard cleared his throat and said firmly, "No. He speaks only of the Christian life and the trials and troubles we all face as we try to obey God's Word. There's nothing sneaky about him."

"There, see, Edmund?" offered Richard's uncle with relief. "What did I tell you? Bunyan's just a preacher."

"Well, be that as it may. You are to keep him inside the Bedford county jail from now on. No exceptions! You understand?"

❖ ❖ ❖

That afternoon Richard and his uncle returned to their work in the jail. Richard was busy scrubbing the walls, attempting to remove some of the damp, musty smell from his uncle's work space when John White said to him, "Well, Richard, I guess I had better tell John Bunyan about Wylde's visit. Can't put it off forever."

With his brush in his hand, Richard followed his uncle to the preacher's cell and listened while John White broke the news to Bunyan. He spoke in a matter-of-fact tone of voice, downplaying the importance of his message. "Bunyan, I have received orders not to let you out of the jail for any purpose at any time . . . from here on out. So, no more trips. Understand?"

John Bunyan stood there staring at the jailer through the bars of his cell door with his mouth slightly open. He glanced over at Richard, who turned away and pretended to clean the wall. But of course, his mind was totally on the conversation between his uncle and John Bunyan.

"I'm sorry, John," said the jailer, "but that's just the way it is."

"But why? Who gave you this order?"

"The sheriff brought word from the magistrates, John. It's their ruling, and there's no way of getting around it."

"But what are they trying to do? How did the magistrates find out?"

"I don't know, John. Apparently, someone's been informing them about your activities, and they are all in a tizzy about them."

"But why?"

"Don't ask me! I don't know. They seldom trouble themselves with matters as small as this, but someone has been telling them what you've been doing, and so I guess they feel obliged to respond."

"But who would tell them? Who cares?"

"Don't speak to me as though I were on trial. I don't know, but obviously someone who knows about your activities has something to gain by reporting them to the authorities."

"You speak as though the person were a traitor, but what is there to betray?"

"I'm not sure, John," said the jailer in exasperation, "but they suspect you of being a conspirator against the king. So they don't want you going off to any more of your meetings. There's nothing I can do about it."

Without further comment, John White turned and went back to his office. Richard also walked away and didn't see Bunyan again until the next morning. But by then the clampdown had done more than restrict his activities. It had dampened his mood as well.

At first Richard tried to stay away from him. The gray look to his skin and the haunted stare in his eyes scared the boy. But when he walked by the old tinker who was again busy at his workbench in the common room, the man reached up and grabbed his sleeve. "What else do you know, lad? Did they say any more yesterday?"

Instinctively, Richard pulled away. "No, nothing that I can remember. What's the matter with you?"

"I guess I'm worried. They arrested me to stop me from preaching without a license. Until now, I considered this imprisonment something of a tug-a-war. I've been insisting on the freedom to preach, but my opponents were not willing to grant me a license. Now it seems as if they are out for blood, saying that I am some kind of conspirator or something. That could get me hung."

"Oh, I don't think so," protested Richard. "If you stay here in the jail, they know you can't do anything against the king from here."

"But last night I had a dream," Bunyan continued in a thin, far-off-sounding voice. "In it I kept seeing the old gallows out at the Caxton crossroads— I've passed it a hundred times in my life. In my dream, I was mounting the steps to have the rope put around my neck. But then my knees seemed to give way, and I started to beg for mercy like a common coward. I've prayed for courage. If I must die, I don't want to die a coward. It would be a denial of Christ, the very hope I've preached to others."

"You need to tell yourself one of those Pilgrim stories," Richard suggested, trying to draw Bunyan out of his dark brooding. "Pilgrim would never let himself be defeated by a thing like this."

"I guess you're right," said John Bunyan with a wry grin. He brushed a strand of limp brown hair back out of his face. "I need to get my eyes on the Heavenly City."

But the next time Richard passed with a bundle of straw in his arms, Bunyan stopped him again. "This is more than a struggle with my own fears," he said urgently. "I'm ready to stay in this jail as long as they want to keep me here. But what about my wife and poor children—especially dear Mary. I can't leave her in the world alone, unable to see. If I were to be put to death, what would she do?"

Richard felt uncomfortable with such questions. How was he supposed to answer them? How was he to comfort a grown man, a preacher at that? He thought again of his father in prison. Maybe if he tried to help the person God put before him, God would send someone to comfort and encourage his own father. "Mary? Why, she'd do just fine," Richard said, not knowing if that would help, but believing it was true, nonetheless. "No one's pluckier than she is. You don't have to worry about her."

John Bunyan smiled faintly. For the moment, Richard's words did seem to give him some encouragement.

The next day when Bunyan's wife, Elizabeth, and daughter, Mary, came by the jail with his food, Richard noticed them talking urgently together in quiet voices. Elizabeth was at least ten years younger than her husband, only about twenty or twenty-two—a second wife. Her golden hair—a stark contrast from her stepdaughter's dark tresses—was mostly hidden under a plain white cap.

Then Richard realized that Bunyan was calling him over to them.

"Richard," the tinker said matter of factly. "I've got to get these charges against me dropped. I'm not willing to promise to never preach again—that would be going against God's instructions—but there may be some legal steps I can take. I wasn't legally charged when I was arrested. If Elizabeth can deliver a petition of acquittal to Lord Barkwood at the House of Lords in London, I might be released."

He looked fondly at his young wife. "But it's not proper for a woman to travel alone. However, if you were to go to London with her, Richard . . . would you be willing?"

Chapter 8

The Petition to Lord Barkwood

A s RICHARD WINSLOW and Elizabeth Bunyan rode in the public coach toward London, Elizabeth reviewed the events that had led up to her husband's arrest. Richard listened intently; it was a story he had not heard before.

When Charles II had returned to power more than a year earlier, the laws of England began to change. Fearing that someone would try to stir up another revolution and throw him out of power as Oliver Cromwell had thrown his father out, King Charles decided to restrict public meetings where revolutionaries might organize and communicate their ideas. In one sense, he had good reason to be afraid because there was a secret group calling itself the Fifth Monarchy that was plotting to remove the king.

But it was not so easy to prohibit all public meetings, so the king decided to try to control what happened in meetings. Therefore, the government required all preachers to be licensed by the Church of England. This, the king thought, would silence anyone with revolutionary tendencies. As a result of this law, the free meetings of the nonconformist believers were restricted or stopped because they had no preachers licensed by the state.

Since John Bunyan was one of these unlicensed preachers, he had been warned that he could no longer preach on the streets of Bedford or in the small churches that met in various homes around the countryside because he had no license. "Stick to being a tinker," he was told, "and let the official clergy tend to the preaching." Bunyan, of course, believed no government had the right to prohibit him from carrying out God's command to preach the Gospel. God's law came first, then human laws.

So, when he was invited on November 12, 1660, to preach at a friend's farm some thirteen miles south of Bedford, he eagerly accepted. But when he got there, the group of believers gathered in the old farmhouse were strangely subdued. Finally, his friend took him aside and said, "John, there is a warrant out for your arrest if you preach here tonight. I happen to know that the constable will not be here for another hour; maybe we ought to dismiss the meeting and all go home."

"By no means," John had said firmly. "I will preach the Word as God has commanded me." Then he turned to the whole group and said more loudly, "Come, let's all cheer up. It is time to praise the Lord."

And so the service began as scheduled.

Before long, the constable arrived, and as expected, he interrupted the meeting and searched everyone present. He was a little apologetic when he found no weapons—these people were not the dangerous revolutionaries his superiors had told him he might find there. But he had his warrant, so he arrested John Bunyan as he had been told to do.

The next morning, Bunyan was brought before a local magistrate, Francis Wingate, for a hearing. Wingate was a hard-nosed man with a chip on his shoulder, but some of Bunyan's friends convinced him to give Bunyan a second chance. "See if you can get him to promise not to preach, and then let him go," they urged.

So Wingate questioned Bunyan and asked him if he would promise to quit preaching.

Bunyan said no, he would never make such a promise. This angered Wingate. Who did this country tinker think he was to reject leniency and refuse to promise to obey the law! In his anger, Wingate sent Bunyan off to the Bedford county jail—not for having preached the night before, but for refusing to promise not to preach again. After that there were other efforts to secure Bunyan's release, but they all required his agreement not to preach anymore, which he steadfastly refused to promise.

When his case finally came to trial in January, the technical charge against him did not involve his preaching at all. Instead, the indictment accused him of "not coming to church to hear divine service" —meaning the official Church of England—but rather taking part in "several unlawful meetings"— meaning the unofficial house churches.

Normally, sentencing did not take place until an accused person pled *guilty* or—if he or she pled *not guilty*—until a trial proved the person guilty. However, in John's case, he avoided pleading either guilty or not guilty by engaging the judges in an argument about what the charge against him actually meant. He pointed out that he regularly did attend church, and told about the worship services he and his fellow Christians often held. The judges then got sidetracked into trying to prove that Bunyan's church wasn't a real church. In the end, the exasperated judges simply sentenced him to prison until he would promise to not preach anymore.

Therefore, Elizabeth pointed out to Richard, John Bunyan had been arrested for something other than what he was charged with and sentenced without having been convicted.

"On the basis of these legal mistakes," she said, holding on to the window ledge of the swaying coach, "John is being held in jail illegally. I intend to petition Lord Barkwood at the House of Lords for his acquittal."

Richard listened admiringly. He was as eager to help secure John Bunyan's release as he was to see his father again.

In London, Elizabeth Bunyan and Richard stayed with Elder Barnabas, the same elder of the secret Puritan church where he and Bunyan had stayed on their first trip. That night Elizabeth told some of the church people all that had happened in Bedford, especially how John's freedom of travel had been restricted and that his enemies seemed to be getting bolder. "We can't figure how John's enemies heard that he had so much freedom. It's as though someone informed them," she said.

The members of the church looked knowingly at one another. "Things have been getting worse here in the city, too," said one of the men. "There is a secret society calling itself the Fifth Monarchy. . . ." At the mention of the group, Richard paid particular attention. There would be no falling asleep for him during this meeting. He had to know who these Puritans were. "Anyway," continued the man, "those Fifth Monarchy people have brought much trouble to all true believers. They claim to be religious, but they really are revolutionaries."

"My John has been accused of being associated with them, but what makes them revolutionaries?" asked Elizabeth.

"Well," said Elder Barnabas, eager to instruct his

country friends with the latest news from the big city, "it's their notion that all earthly kings should be overthrown so they can take over. They say that the Assyrians, Persians, Greeks, and Romans were the first four monarchies, and now it is time for Christ to come back to earth and reign for a thousand years. Of course, *they* are the ones to set up this new government."

"Well, we are to expect Christ's return," said Elizabeth innocently.

"Yes, but these rascals would take over the country by force. Not long ago they started a riot here in London in which many people were killed. The government is truly afraid of them."

The more Richard listened to this conversation, the more assured he became that John Bunyan and these Christians had nothing to do with anything revolutionary.

"The problem is," continued Elder Barnabas, "many people accuse us Puritans of being part of this group like they did your John. It has put pressure on us all."

The next day, when Elizabeth Bunyan went to meet with Lord Barkwood, Richard set out to visit his father.

However, instead of going straight to the imposing prison, he stopped by his family's old house.

Everything was dark and shut up as he expected.

He snuck around to the back and quietly let himself in the rear door with his key. There was a strange musty smell to the quiet house that did not remind him at all of home.

He crept through the kitchen and into the hall and was just passing the library when a pitiful yell came from the room, followed by a loud crash. Richard spun on his heels to make his escape when out of the corner of his eye he saw old Walter, the butler, sprawled on the floor try-

ing to get his feet back under himself.

"Walter, what are you doing down there?" he gasped.

As the old man pulled himself up by the back of a chair and shakily regained a nearly upright stance, he blubbered, "I might be asking you much the same thing, young man. Why are you here without so much as a civil warning? You nearly frightened me to death."

"I didn't mean to frighten you," said Richard, hurrying forward to assist the old man. "I'm sorry. I guess—" Suddenly he stopped. Why should he have to issue a warning before entering his own house? "I'm sorry I frightened you," he finished simply.

Walter sat down in the chair that he had used to help himself up and took several deep breaths.

"Why don't you have some light in here? Then I'd have known you were home."

"Where else would I be?" the old man grouched. Then he waved his hand as though to dismiss the question. "I don't use lights because I don't wish to attract any attention to the house. Things are bad, Master Richard," said the butler. "When I heard you in the hall, I thought you might be the king's men come for me. I guess I tripped over something." He peered at the dark floor to see what might have caught his foot. "I expect them any day, you know. You should not be here in the city."

Richard stayed within the darkened old house most of the morning trying to rally his courage enough to go to the Tower. He really didn't want to go to that awful place, but—his father was there, and maybe if he went he could help his father in some way. Besides, what had his father been saying the last time he had visited—something about Cromwell being able to prove that he didn't belong in the Tower?

Richard reviewed that conversation over and over in his mind, but he couldn't make any sense of it. What difference could Cromwell make? He was dead.

It was afternoon before Richard emerged from the old house and headed toward the Tower. As was his custom, he came out the back door, ran down the alley, then ducked between two buildings to emerge on the street. He walked briskly up the block with his shoulders hunched and head down, hoping that no one would recognize him. He peered this way and that out of the corners of his eyes, and then, just as he turned the corner, he caught a glimpse of someone half a block behind him. The figure ducked out of sight into an alcove along a garden wall—but why? Richard knew that wall well. There was an old gate there, but it hadn't been used for years.

The person had no reasonable business turning in there. It was simply someplace out of his sight. *But why hide from me?* Richard wondered. The obvious answer was, he was being followed!

Chapter 9

Shadows in the Alleys

RICHARD DASHED DOWN THE STREET and skidded to a stop as he rounded the corner. Was the man really following him? This was no time to get carried away with unreasonable fears. It was his chance to visit his father.

He returned to the corner and peeked around. There came the same stranger at a brisk walk. He was young, and though he did not look like a nobleman, he was dressed better than the average working man. Long, curly, dark hair tumbled down below a large-brimmed hat pinned up on one side with a sweeping red feather. His waistcoat and breeches were

95

dark green, his hose burgundy. *At least*, thought Richard, *those bucket-topped boots of his won't let him run very fast*. But the man kept coming at a quick pace, turning his head right and left, obviously looking for someone as he hurried along.

He's looking for me! There's no question. Richard lost no time and took off at a run.

When he got to the Thames, he headed east along the river until he came to London Bridge. He would have darted across it, but the drawbridge was up. So he slid behind a wagon filled with wine barrels to see if his pursuer was still on his trail.

Richard wasn't far from the Tower; maybe he ought to run straight there. Certainly this man, whoever he was, couldn't follow him within its walls—that is, not unless the man was a government official, and the whole plan was to catch him and take him to the Tower, too.

Just then, he saw the man's dark hat with the red feather bobbing along through the people waiting for the bridge to open. Richard took off running again, past the Tower and on along the river until he came to the Docklands. There he made his way between the warehouses and through the alleys until he was sure he had lost his "shadow."

All afternoon he was afraid to go out on the main streets or return to the Tower for fear his pursuer would be waiting for him. He hid until dark, then made his way by a longer route back to Elder Barnabas's house, his opportunity to see his father lost.

When he knocked on the door and was admitted, he realized that Elizabeth Bunyan had arrived only a few minutes before him because she was still removing her cloak. Their host invited both guests into the simple dining room where crocks of thick soup were brought and placed before them. It seemed that there were always several people at the elder's house. Richard hadn't yet figured who was a part of the family, who were church members living there, who were overnight guests like himself and Mrs. Bunyan, and who were just visiting for the evening. All seemed to pitch in as though this were their home.

Two women and an old man crowded into the room and sat at the table while Richard and Mrs. Bunyan ate. Elder Barnabas came and stood in the doorway. Looking directly at Richard, he said, "Well, give us a report. What did you accomplish today?"

"Not much," sighed Elizabeth, thinking he was speaking only to her, which he might have been, but at the time Richard had felt that the man had been asking *him* to give an account of his day. In any case, Elizabeth looked up at the elder and continued. "I had to wait several hours before I had an opportunity to speak to Lord Barkwood. Finally, I caught him in the hall as he was coming out of some committee meeting."

With a gasp, one of the women said, "What was he like?"

"Oh, my. I'd be much too timid to speak to a lord, especially right in the House of Lords," said the other woman.

"Quiet down, now," said Elder Barnabas. "I'm sure we all admire Mrs. Bunyan's courage, but let's give her a chance to tell us what happened. Please continue." He nodded to Elizabeth.

"Well, there's not much more to say. He was courteous enough, but once I explained the situation, he said there was nothing he could do—"

"What do you mean?" Richard butted in. "I thought a lord could do just about anything."

Elizabeth shrugged. "I had hoped so, but Lord Barkwood said that if John was wrongfully arrested, then we needed to get the circuit court in Bedford to rule on the matter. It would not be proper for him to interfere."

A quiet moan of disappointment escaped those in the small room. "I am sorry your petition didn't produce any fruit," said the old man. "But you certainly are a brave person to attempt this for your husband."

"Yes," said the woman closest to Richard. "To go right to the House of Lords and wait for Lord Barkwood. Why, that's as brave as Daniel walking into the lion's den."

"My, yes," said the other woman. "And to think that you traveled all the way here by yourself. I admire you, Mrs. Bunyan."

Wait a minute, thought Richard. *She didn't travel here by herself. I came with her. Don't I count?* But he wasn't feeling like he counted for much. The more everyone admired Elizabeth Bunyan for what she had done that day, the more Richard began to feel like a coward for having given up on visiting his father. His thoughts spun off to the streets of London and the shadowy person who had been following him.

Suddenly, he realized that Mrs. Bunyan was speaking to him. "I say, Richard, how did you find your father today?"

"How?" he mumbled, thinking at first that she was asking how he found his way to the Tower. But obviously she was asking whether his father was all right. "Oh . . . well, he is doing as well as can be expected—for being in prison."

He hoped she wouldn't ask more, but she pressed on. "Is there any news of his release?"

"No. Things are about the same," he mumbled, then quickly changed the subject. "I say, is there any more of this soup?"

His face felt hot, and he was certain that he must be blushing with embarrassment. He had just told a lie, causing everyone to think he had visited his father when, in fact, he hadn't had the courage to go to the Tower at all.

More soup came, but he couldn't eat it.

Soon the little group was busy talking about other things, but Richard couldn't help but think that Elder Barnabas was looking at him very closely. *Somehow he knows,* thought Richard. *He knows that I didn't go to the Tower.* But there didn't seem to be anything he could do about it at the moment.

The trip back to Bedford was grim. The day was dark and rainy, and Richard and Elizabeth's spirits were gray. What was going to happen to their loved ones? The question hung over both of them like the stormy clouds in the sky, and there didn't seem to be much reason to talk about it.

The coach was a fast one in spite of the rain, and they arrived that evening. Together they went to the Bedford jail, sloshing through the muddy streets with their wraps pulled tightly around them.

In the jail, John Bunyan greeted them hopefully. And even when Elizabeth reported her failure to get any help from Lord Barkwood, he was still able to say, "The Lord knows our need. He will provide." Then Bunyan turned to Richard. "And how did your visit with your father go?"

Having already told a lie that Elizabeth Bunyan had heard, Richard repeated it by saying his father was satisfactory. Then he added, "He is well, but I think he is losing hope for any release."

"I'm sorry to hear that," said John Bunyan. "Very sorry. But we must not despair. Here, sit down and have a piece of my bread. Let me tell you another Pilgrim story that I've been thinking about. Maybe it will revive your spirits. Elizabeth, you can stay a few minutes, can't you?"

They sat together on the straw, and a few other prisoners gathered around. John Bunyan's stories were becoming a valued form of entertainment in the jail.

"On his journey to the Heavenly City," began

Bunyan, "Pilgrim picked up a worthy companion named Hopeful. But one day they strayed off their path and nearly became lost. Before they recovered, a storm hit—much like the one raging outside this evening." Bunyan gestured toward the small window through which they could hear that the rain was coming down much harder.

Finding an old shed, Pilgrim and Hopeful crawled into the rough shelter and soon fell asleep.

Now, not far from the place where they lay, there was a castle called Doubting Castle. It was owned by Giant Despair. Unknown to our two travelers, it was his property where they were now sleeping.

When morning broke, Giant Despair got up early and went for a walk in his fields. There he caught Pilgrim and Hopeful asleep in his small shed. He picked them up with his mighty hands and with a grim voice said, "Wake up, you vagabonds! Where are you from?"

"We are Pilgrim and Hopeful," answered Pilgrim, "and we are on our way to the Heavenly City, but in the storm last night we lost our way and were waiting out the weather before continuing on."

The giant said, "Well, you have trespassed on my property, trampling through my fields. Therefore you must go along with me."

So they were forced to go, because he was so much stronger than they. They also didn't have anything to say because they knew they were at fault.

The giant carried them to his castle as though they where rats and threw them into a dark dungeon, very nasty and stinking. Here they lay from Wednesday morning till Saturday night without one bit of bread or a drop to drink or any light.

Giant Despair had a wife named Distrust-ful. When he went to bed, he told her what he had done. "What do you think I should do with them?"

"You should beat them mercilessly. We can't trust any strangers," she said.

In the morning, he went to the dungeon and at first started calling them dogs. Then he beat them until they couldn't rise.

That night Distrustful told Giant Despair that he ought to kill them. But when he went to do so the next morning, he had a fit and couldn't use his hands. Fortunately for the travelers, he staggered out of the dungeon without hurting them worse.

But they were so shaken by what he had planned to do that they wondered if it would be better if they took their own lives rather than wait for him to torture them to death.

"Brother," said Pilgrim, "what shall we do? Is it better to live to be tortured or die at our own hand? It seems to me that the grave would be better than this dungeon."

"Indeed, our present condition is dread-ful," said Hopeful, "and death would be wel-come. But what would God say? He said, 'Thou shalt do no murder.' Certainly that applies to killing ourselves. And Giant Despair doesn't always have the last word. God is still in charge, and others have made it out of this dungeon. Maybe the giant will die or forget to lock us in. As long as there is life, there is hope. Let us not be our own murderers."

For the time, that restored their courage.

But when night came, the giant's wife asked him about the prisoners.

"They are sturdy rascals," he said. "They would rather bear all hardship than to take their own lives."

"Tomorrow take them into the castle yard and show them the bones and skulls of those you have already killed. Then they will give up rather than wait for you to tear them in pieces."

So in the morning, the giant took Pilgrim and Hopeful to the castle yard. "This is what happened to other travelers whom I caught on my land. I tore them in pieces, and so I will do to you." Then he beat them all the way back to the dungeon.

In their misery, the travelers renewed their conversation about giving up and bringing an end to it all by taking their own lives. But about midnight, they began to pray, and continued in prayer till almost break of day.

Now, a little before daybreak, Pilgrim suddenly sat up and said, "What a fool I have been. I have a key in my pocket, called Promise, that will, I am sure, open any lock in Doubting Castle."

"Well, let's try it," said Hopeful.

And when they did, they discovered that

the key called Promise did indeed open the door of their dungeon. Out they walked and continued on all night until, by morning, they were back on the King's highway on the way to the Heavenly City.

As John Bunyan finished his story, there were murmurs of appreciation and a little clapping from several of the prisoners as they rose to be about the little tasks by which they passed the time in jail.

But not Richard. He was looking around dumbfounded. "Wait a minute," he blurted. "I thought these Pilgrim stories were about truth—allegories, you called them—but that's not realistic." He looked around at the ragged men and women of the Bedford jail. "None of you carries a key around your neck that will open these doors. And neither does my father," said Richard, feeling like the story somehow mocked the seriousness of his father's plight.

John Bunyan lowered his head slightly, then spoke in a gentle voice. "I was not speaking of these stone walls" —he gestured around him— "or the Tower in London, young Richard. Instead, I was referring to another dungeon many of us have been in and out of more than once during our time in this jail, a dungeon in which I sensed you were in danger of being trapped even now. And for that prison we do carry a key."

"What do you mean?"

"The giant in the story was named Giant *Despair*. His wife was *Distrustful*. And the pilgrims were

105

caught in the dungeon of *Doubting* Castle. There is only one key out of such a trap. Not even the giant himself could have freed poor Pilgrim and Hopeful."

"Why not?"

"Because the key out of despair and discouragement is not something any human can do for you. In fact, you can't even get out yourself. Wishful thinking is of no value."

"I don't understand," said Richard. "You said they had the key."

"Indeed. But it had been given to them. It was not something they created. The key was the promise that they had received, a promise that has been given to each of us."

"What promise?"

"God's promise. The promise in the Bible that says, 'And we know that all things work together for good to them that love God.' "

Richard's eyes drifted slowly toward the heavy oak door of the jail.

"No, Richard," said Bunyan. "It won't open *that* door, but it will open the door in here." He patted his chest. Then he gestured toward both Richard and Elizabeth. "When the two of you came in here tonight, I was afraid that the door of despair was closing on you. I hope you'll use the promise 'key' to keep it open."

"Thank you, John," said Elizabeth, her cheeks flushed. "It's true, I was very discouraged." She gave her husband a kiss. "We'll try, but right now I need to get home to the children. Poor Mary has taken care of them for four days. And I'm sure Richard needs to get to bed, too. I'll see you tomorrow."

Richard rose obediently, not daring to speak. How did John Bunyan know he was close to despair?—not only at his father's imprisonment, but at his own cowardice that kept him from seeing his father when he had a chance.

Chapter 10

The Battle in the Swan Chamber

THAT NIGHT IN BED, Richard thought about Bunyan's story and the Promise. Suddenly, what had sounded like a riddle at the time became clear to him. If God was really in control of all things, and if He had made a promise that everything would work out for those who loved Him, then there wasn't any reason to despair and feel discouraged.

Things might *seem* to be going badly, but God would take care of the final outcome. But the more Richard thought about God, the more uncomfortable he became. He had lied about visiting his father, both to Elizabeth and Elder Barnabas in London and to John Bunyan. It was such a little lie, slipping out of his mouth like wiggling fish from his hand. He knew God didn't like lying, but how was he to get back that lie? It seemed gone forever.

Would God keep His promises to someone who lied?

Three days passed before Richard saw Mrs. Bunyan again.

"Well, Richard," Elizabeth said as she arrived at the jail with the little jug of soup that Mary normally delivered, "I've decided to take John's advice and not give in to despair. I'm going to trust God to care for John." She was wearing a plain gray dress that brought out the blue in her eyes.

Richard smiled without much enthusiasm, and Elizabeth perceived his skepticism. "That doesn't mean I'm going to quit doing what I can do. I'm going to try to get John Bunyan a hearing in the local circuit court."

Doing something—almost anything—seemed like a good idea to Richard. By then he was feeling pretty low. Not only had he been a coward, but he had lied to cover it up. *Maybe I can also do something that would make up for my lies,* he thought. *Then maybe the Promise would be mine.*

"Could I help you, Mrs. Bunyan?" he asked.

"I suppose. All I can do right now is deliver some

petitions to the judges of the circuit court. They are in town right now, so I'm going to ask them to grant John a hearing. But I'd be glad for you to come along. Do you have some time this afternoon?"

"Soon as I get a couple buckets of fresh water," he said.

When Richard finished his chores, he and Elizabeth Bunyan headed down High Street to Guildhall, which served as the county courthouse when court was in session. Within it they found Sir Matthew Hale, one of the judges who would rule on John Bunyan if he were granted a hearing. Sir Matthew had served as a judge under Cromwell and was therefore inclined to grant a sympathetic ear to religious dissenters.

Sir Matthew had a pale, gentle face from which his deep-set eyes gave a somewhat sad expression beneath dark eyebrows. He glanced over the paper that Elizabeth handed him. "You are, I take it, Mrs. Bunyan?"

"Yes, my lord," Elizabeth said with a small nod of her head.

"And is this your brother?" said Sir Matthew, glancing at Richard. "You appear far too young to have a son of this age."

"Oh no, my lord. He's neither son nor brother." Elizabeth turned to Richard to let him speak for himself.

"I am Richard Winslow. I work for my uncle, John White. He's the jailer."

"Ye-e-s-s" —Sir Matthew drew the word out as he

rubbed his clean-shaven chin— "John White. He's rather too lenient, I'm told. I wouldn't think working in a jail is a suitable place for a young boy such as yourself. Is that why he grants so many liberties to his prisoners—to make the place more pleasant?"

"I don't think so, sir," Richard said, but added nothing more. *Better to say little and be thought a fool than to say too much and prove it so*, he thought, remembering his father's advice whenever important guests came to the house.

"Well, never mind." Sir Matthew looked back at Elizabeth and smiled slightly. "I will consider your petition, madam, and do my best for you."

With that, he put aside the petition and picked up some other papers. Richard and Elizabeth realized that their meeting was over.

The next day Elizabeth and Richard went looking for another judge, Sir Thomas Twisden. "He's not going to be so agreeable," said Elizabeth. "They say he's a hanging judge, quick to give out the harshest sentences. But we must give him a copy of this petition because he will also sit on the bench if John is granted a hearing."

When they stopped by the courthouse, a clerk said Judge Twisden was having lunch at the Swan Inn. But as they went down the street and approached the inn, they saw an older man come out of the building fancily dressed in a long red coat trimmed with white fur. He had a heavy, fat face with a large red nose and a mouth that turned down at the edges in a permanent frown. Gray, stringy hair fell to his shoulders.

"Sir Thomas!" called Elizabeth loudly enough for him to easily hear at the forty-foot distance. "Sir Thomas Twisden, I must give you something."

But the man didn't even look in their direction. Instead, he climbed into his ornate carriage and ordered the coachman to drive away.

Richard grabbed the petition and ran after the carriage, which was not heading over the bridge but was in the act of making a U-turn to head back up High Street. Richard easily overtook it before it finished its turn and threw the petition in through its open window.

In a glance, Judge Twisden saw what the paper was and threw it out of his coach, yelling back, "He'll not be released unless he promises to stop preaching."

As Richard walked back toward the forlorn wife of the jailed preacher, he said, "How are we ever going to get him to consider the petition?"

"I don't know," she sighed, "but we can't give up. God will just have to make a way." But Richard noticed that there were tears in her eyes.

While they were standing in the middle of the street, not knowing what to do next, Sheriff Edmund Wylde came out of the Swan Inn. Richard recognized him immediately as the man he had shared a coach with when he first came to Bedford and who had come by the jail some time later to tell his uncle that John Bunyan was not to be allowed any more unusual liberties. "I saw what happened," the sheriff said as he approached Elizabeth and Richard. "Don't mind him. He's a sour old goat."

"But I needed to deliver this petition to him," said Elizabeth, smoothing out the crinkled paper Richard had rescued from the street.

"Really? What do you have there?" said the sheriff. He read it over, then said, "Don't give up. This evening when court is adjourned, both Judge Hale and Judge Twisden will probably be right up there." The sheriff turned and pointed to the window of an upper room in the Swan Inn. "They usually meet with several of the local gentry to review the day's court proceedings and discuss other business of the shire."

"But how should we ever be admitted to the Swan Chamber?" asked Elizabeth, naming the classy dining room to which the sheriff referred.

"Oh, I wouldn't worry about that," said the sheriff with a wink. "I imagine someone as pretty as you could walk straight in there. The worst they can do is tell you to leave. In the meantime, you might get a chance to make your request."

Richard had waited in the town square all afternoon while Elizabeth went home to care for the children. While he waited, he had seen Sir Thomas Twisden return in his carriage and go into the courthouse. Then, when court was over, both judges and several other men came out and walked down the street to the Swan Inn, just as the sheriff had said they would. As time passed, others went in as well.

Richard hardly recognized Elizabeth when she arrived. She wore the same plain gray dress, but she had put on a clean white collar and cuffs and had brushed her hair into a knot at the back of her head from which beautiful golden ringlets fell.

"Let's pray," she said when she got to where Richard was standing. Richard bowed his head and listened respectfully as the young woman said, "O Lord, you know John is innocent of all wrongdoing. He was only trying to serve and obey you. Please grant us courage now as we plea for justice. But more importantly, let your will be done."

She took Richard's arm as they walked toward the inn. He could feel that she was trembling, but her step was sure and steady. Just inside the door, she quickly guided Richard toward some stairs. They followed a barmaid up the steps as she carried a basket of bread in one hand and a large pitcher of beer in the other. "Let me through. Clear a way," said the barmaid to those who blocked the steps and the interior of the dining room.

By following closely behind the maid, Richard and Elizabeth managed to get all the way to the main table where both judges and several other gentlemen sat in conversation.

"My lord," Elizabeth began in a clear, loud voice as she addressed Sir Matthew Hale. "I come to you again to ask your lordship what can be done for my husband."

The conversation stopped, and all the important men of Bedford looked up at her.

"Woman," said Sir Matthew in a much less friendly tone than he had used the day before in the courthouse. "Your husband pled guilty. There's nothing I can do to help him."

"My lord, that is not so. He did not plead guilty. He was only answering questions put to him about the *nature* of the charge against him."

Suddenly, Judge Twisden interrupted with a face red with anger. "Do you think we can do what we want? Your husband is a lawbreaker, and we are bound to uphold the law. Even if we wanted to, we couldn't release him. And I, for one, certainly have no desire to release him until he agrees to quit preaching. Why, just the other day, our justice of the peace, Sir Henry Chester, reported to me that Jailer White was giving this man special liberties. But did he use them to spend time with his family? No. He ran off to preach in London. Sir Henry actually saw the man in London. But I wonder, was it preaching he did there or conspiring with those revolutionaries calling themselves the Fifth Monarchy? This man belongs in jail."

"But my lords, he was not lawfully convicted," said Elizabeth, gaining confidence. Then she told about going to London and speaking with Lord Barkwood. At the mention of a member of the House of Lords, the judges became far more attentive. "Lord Barkwood advised me to petition you for a proper trial. So I am here on his advice."

There was a moment of silence. Then Judge Twisden said, "Will he quit preaching?"

Elizabeth's shoulders sank. "My lord, he will not quit preaching as long as he is able to speak."

"Then why are we wasting our time on such a fellow?" And he grabbed his flagon of beer as though the matter was over.

But Judge Hale turned to some of the other men and said, "What's this man's occupation, anyway?"

Several spoke up at once, saying that he was just a tinker, though all agreed a good one. At that, Judge Hale also turned away as though the issue was over.

But Elizabeth was not ready to give up. "Is it because he is a tinker that there is no justice for a poor man in England?"

Her words seemed to strike a nerve. England prided itself on its system of justice—as unjust as it sometimes was.

"That's not the point," said Sir Matthew in a much more kindly tone. "It's just that because his statements were recorded as a confession of guilt, he is considered guilty. There is nothing we can do, madam. Maybe he could apply to the king for a pardon. I am truly sorry. Now leave us in peace."

Elizabeth did not move for a full minute. Then, realizing there was nothing more she could say, she turned and followed Richard down the steps into the darkening street.

Chapter 11

Letter From the Past

THE NEXT DAY, RICHARD RETURNED to his work at the jail with a heavy heart. It was not just that Elizabeth Bunyan had failed to secure a new hearing for her husband. It was that things *didn't* seem to be working out for good according to the Promise. *If God won't rescue someone noble and good like John Bunyan from trouble, what hope do I have for things turning out good for me and my father?* he wondered. The memory of his lie continued to trouble him.

Later that day, a thick letter arrived at the Bedford jail addressed to John Bunyan. Richard delivered it and thought nothing  more about it until that afternoon when Mary brought her father's jug of soup.

Richard let her into Bunyan's cell and started to go on about his work when the tinker said, "Richard, when Mary leaves, could you stay a few minutes? Something arrived in the mail that I want to discuss with you."

Richard shrugged agreeably and went on about his duties, but he kept wondering what could have come in Bunyan's letter that involved him.

Once Richard had said good-bye to Mary and returned to Bunyan, the preacher said, "Richard, is there any chance that you have lied to me in the past?"

A wave of shock rolled over him. How could John Bunyan have found out that he hadn't visited his father? For certainly that must be the lie that Bunyan wondered about. It was the only lie he had ever told the prisoner.

But just as he was ready to confess, the thought struck him that maybe Bunyan *didn't* know about his not visiting his father. Maybe he was asking about something else entirely, something that had not been a lie. So Richard approached the subject cautiously. "Why do you ask?" he said, hoping he could wiggle out of admitting his untruthfulness.

"The letter I received today came from London, and it caused me to wonder."

Richard's heart sank. Somehow John Bunyan had learned the truth. There was nothing to do but come clean. With deep embarrassment, Richard said, "I didn't . . . I mean, I didn't mean to," he stumbled. Then he blurted it all out in one stream. "It's just that when Mrs. Bunyan asked me, I said yes, and Elder Barnabas heard me, so when you asked me, I had to say the same thing to you."

"You lost me in a swirl of snowflakes, lad. What did Elizabeth ask you? And what did you say yes to?"

Slowly, Richard made his confession. He had not visited his father on his last trip to London because someone was following him, and he was afraid. "Everyone was making so much over how brave Mrs. Bunyan was when she went to talk to Lord Barkwood, I was ashamed to admit that I got scared and didn't go see my father."

"I thought as much," mumbled Bunyan, shaking his head. "Well, if you didn't visit him, what did you do?"

"I hid." Seeing the puzzlement on Bunyan's face, he explained. "I was going to see him, but Walter said it was very dangerous, so . . ."

"Wait a minute, wait a minute. Who is this Walter chap—a friend of yours? And where did you meet him?"

"Walter is our family butler. I went by our house— he still lives there—and nearly scared him to death. He said it was very dangerous in London these days. When I left to see my father, I was very wary. And sure enough, someone started following me. I ran and ran until I finally got away. But then I had to hide in an alley in Dockland. By the time it was safe to go back on the main streets, it was too late to go to the Tower. So I returned to the elder's house."

Bunyan nodded somewhat skeptically. "It's not uncommon to lose one's courage, especially in times like these," he admitted, rubbing his forehead with the tips of the fingers of one hand. He looked out of the sides of his eyes at Richard and said, "I have one more question, Richard. Were you the one who told the magistrates about my liberties from jail? Did you report to one of them how John White was letting me out from time to time?"

"No, never!" Richard protested. "I didn't say anything to anyone."

"You know that someone reported to them about my travels, don't you? You were here when the sheriff came and told your uncle to end such liberties, remember? At first, it seemed as though we had a traitor among our church brothers and sisters. But maybe it was you. Were you the one who gave me away?"

"No, no! It wasn't me. *But I know who it was,*" said Richard. He felt suddenly relieved as he remembered something that had been said in the Swan Chamber the day before. "It was Sir Henry Chester, the local justice of the peace. He knows about everything that happens here in Bedford. And yesterday in the Swan Chamber—you can ask Mrs. Bunyan— Sir Thomas Twisden said Sir Henry was the one who reported on you. In fact, when he went to London, he actually saw you there, too. It wasn't me. You've got to believe me."

"I do believe you," said Bunyan with a sigh of relief. "I didn't ever think you would betray me, but when I discovered that you had lied, it naturally caused me to think that I didn't know you as well as I thought I did."

"Yes, sir." Richard hung his head. "I'm sorry. I'm truly sorry for lying." Richard sat silently for a few moments. Then his curiosity got the best of him. "How did you know that I had lied about visiting my father?"

"First of all," said John Bunyan with a broad smile, "let me say that I forgive you. But learn this lesson: 'Be sure your sins will find you out.' That's from the Bible. As to how I discovered your lie, it was that letter you brought me today. It was from Elder Barnabas in London. And you were right; someone was following you around London."

Richard's eyes widened. "Really? Who?"

"When Elizabeth told the believers in London that someone had reported my unusual freedoms, it sounded to Elder Barnabas—as it did to me—like someone had betrayed us. So, Elder Barnabas asked one of his young men to check on you, to see where you went."

"But why? Why would he suspect me?"

"Because he had heard about your father before and therefore had reason to think you might be spying on me."

"My father, Obadiah Winslow?" gasped Richard in bewilderment. "But why my father? What would cause him to think that my father—or I—was a traitor? My father is in the Tower *because* he worked for Oliver Cromwell. That makes him kind of on your side since Cromwell was a Puritan. He's there because the king's men don't trust him. So why would Elder Barnabas doubt us?"

Bunyan held up his hands to calm Richard. "Let me explain," he said. "Apparently, shortly before Oliver Cromwell died, he sent Elder Barnabas a letter asking for advice. Cromwell considered Elder Barnabas his pastor and valued his wisdom. Anyway, Cromwell had discovered that his trusted secretary, Obadiah Winslow—your father—was spying for General George Monck in Scotland. Monck was dedicated to returning Charles II to the throne, which, of course, you know he succeeded in doing two years after Cromwell's death."

Richard was speechless.

"Along with his own letter to me," John Bunyan continued, "Elder Barnabas sent me Cromwell's letter to him concerning your father. This is it." He handed the tattered, yellow sheet to Richard. "There's no doubting it. You can see Cromwell's seal right there on the bottom."

Richard stared at the letter in amazement as John Bunyan continued. "When Elder Barnabas learned you were Obadiah's son, he had reason to be cautious about you, especially when he heard that there seemed to be an informer in our midst. Therefore, this last time when you were in London, he had someone follow you."

"He thought I was meeting with some of the king's men?" asked Richard in surprise. "To report on you and the other believers?"

"He wasn't sure. He was only checking. The man followed you to a strange house, and when you came out several hours later, you ran, finally losing him in the alleys near the docks. Knowing that you said you were going to the Tower to see your father, he went there and waited, but you never showed. Elder Barnabas realized that all of that could have been chance and proved nothing amiss. But later, when you lied, saying that you *had* visited your father, he became even more suspicious."

"But now you know why I didn't visit my father,"

protested Richard.

"True enough," assured Bunyan, putting his hand on the boy's arm. "But at the time, that wasn't clear. We usually lie thinking we will avoid trouble. But in this case, the lie got you into trouble. It caused your actions to *look* suspicious. So, he wrote me to warn me, thinking that if you were an enemy, you might do more damage. He sent Cromwell's letter along as proof and told me to do with it as I please."

Richard again stared at the letter. "So, what are you going to do?" he asked in a small voice.

"I have already forgiven you, and I am satisfied that you did not betray me. There's nothing more . . . except for that letter. It's yours to do with as you please. It was sent to me because of the suspicions your lies created, but now that you have repented, God can use it for good. Do you realize its significance?"

"No."

"Son, that piece of paper is your father's ticket out of prison."

"But . . . how?" asked Richard, bewildered.

John Bunyan leaned back against the cold stone of the jail and looked up at the beamed ceiling. "The winds of change blow to and fro," he said philosophically. "One day we have revolution. The next day the king is back in power." He shrugged and looked Richard in the eye. "I am more interested in eternal things. I feel no malice toward your father no matter which side he took. He probably had his reasons. Cromwell could have hanged him as a traitor. But that was yesterday, and he did not. Who knows why?

"Today, that letter proves your father is no enemy of Charles II. It should get him out of the Tower as soon as you show it to the right people."

Richard looked again at the well-worn paper in his hands. He could hardly comprehend what had just happened. His father—a spy? Richard didn't know what he thought of that—but he did know one thing.

Now his father could be free.

Chapter 12

One Out, One In

WITH A BOUNCE IN HIS STEP, Richard threw his bag over his shoulder the next morning and said good-bye to his Aunt Agnes. The childless woman's round face was blotchy, and her chin quivered as she hugged her nephew good-bye.

Next Richard stopped by the jail where he found his uncle already hard at work. "I guess my vacation is over," his uncle teased as he brought in a load of straw. They talked for a while, then Richard went to speak to some of the prisoners. He especially wanted to thank John Bunyan for providing the letter he hoped would lead to his father's release from jail.

John Bunyan sat on his

little bench in the corner of the ground floor open room. He was not cutting and tagging the laces as he so commonly did, hour after endless hour. Instead, he was leaning slightly to one side so that the light from the small window above him would fall across the pages of his tattered Bible.

Suddenly, Richard was overcome by the contrast between his own situation and that of this country preacher. He stood there bag in hand, ready to ride to London where the prison gates would soon open for his father. But Bunyan sat at his bench in a dingy jail where the heavy doors had recently slammed all the tighter.

At that moment, Bunyan looked up and smiled across the room. "Richard, my boy, come here. I understand you're headed to London today. I'm going to miss you."

Richard went over and dropped his bag to the floor as Bunyan made a space for him to join him on the bench. "I'll miss you, too," said Richard. His voice sounded pinched.

"Say, now, what's troubling you, lad? You don't sound as though this was your day of jubilee."

Richard shrugged, then finally blurted, "I've been thinking, Mr. Bunyan. Remember when you told Mary and me about the Promise, how God will work all things out for good?"

Bunyan nodded and waited for Richard to continue.

"Things are turning out good for me—and my father—but what about you? How can your rotting in jail week after week be good? Nothing seems to be going right for you."

Bunyan grimaced his face and stretched his arms as high into the musty air as he could. "Now that's a tough one," he admitted with a sigh as he ended his stretch. "But who am I to judge what God considers good? We don't always see the end from the beginning."

He turned so that he faced Richard and clapped his hands. "You remember the story about Joseph in the Bible?" Richard nodded, and Bunyan continued. "His brothers sold him into slavery down in Egypt. There Joseph was falsely accused and thrown into prison—for years. Finally he was released and made an important ruler after God helped him interpret the Pharaoh's dreams about the coming famine.

"After suffering for thirteen years, God used Joseph to save the lives of his father, brothers, and their families. And when that happened, do you remember what Joseph said to his brothers?"

Richard shook his head.

"Joseph said, 'You intended evil against me; but God meant it for good.'" John Bunyan stopped and smiled at Richard, waiting for him to catch the point of this ancient story. "Don't you see?" he finally asked. "For thirteen years everything seemed to be going badly, and in fact, the brothers intended it all to be evil. But that wasn't God's view. He used it for good and in the end saved the whole family, a whole nation, even."

"So you're saying," said Richard, "that even

though you are in jail now, God might be making something good come out of it?" He shook his head. "I've worked here long enough to know that jail isn't what you'd call *good* for anyone."

"Don't confuse easy and comfortable with good, lad. I'd be the last one to tell you I enjoy it in here, but I do believe God has me here for a purpose."

Bunyan reached out and put his arm around Richard's shoulder. "I confess," he said, "from our human point of view, things don't look so good for me. But what's 'good,' my boy? How do we measure true goodness? I may want out of prison, but God may want to do something more important by letting me remain here for now . . . though I can't imagine what it might be," he sighed. "I must not let myself be defeated by circumstances!"

The two friends—one young and headed off for more joyous prospects, the other older and locked in jail—looked at each other in silence. Then Bunyan said, "Tell you what, that mail coach of yours won't be in for another hour or so. Why don't you run over to the house and get Mary—it's about time for my soup anyway—and when the two of you get back, I'll tell you both another Pilgrim story. It'll be a kind of going-away gift to you."

At the small Bunyan cottage, six-year-old Johnny flung open the door to let Richard in. Then he ran off to continue his play so quickly that he forgot to close the door until his mother called him back.

Within, Richard found Mrs. Bunyan fanning some damp, barely glowing coals in the family's small fireplace. "Let me help you with that," Richard offered.

"Oh, thank you, Richard," Elizabeth Bunyan said as she got up. "When you get it going, could you swing that pot over the fire? It's time for Mary to take John's soup to him, and it's not even hot. I don't know what's happened to my time this morning."

Richard looked around the room. "Where *is* Mary?"

"She's out back with Thomas. I hear you're on your way back to London."

Richard told her the good news about the letter from Cromwell and the high hopes he had for getting his father out of jail. When he had finished, Elizabeth said, "I'm glad for you." She turned her back to Richard and busied herself with pouring the now-hot soup into the jug. When she turned back around, her voice cracked as she said, "You've been a good friend . . . going with me to London and helping me try to get a hearing for my John. Thank you, Richard, and may God be with you."

She called Mary, put the jug into her step-daughter's hands, hugged Richard briefly, and pushed them both out the door.

The two young people walked in silence. Richard still marveled at how well Mary got around without her eyesight. It was as though she had memorized every tuft of grass, root, and mud puddle on the path to the jail. Not once did she stumble or hesitate.

"Do you really think your father will get out of prison?" said Mary, breaking the silence between them.

"It's almost certain," said Richard excitedly. "The letter your father gave me proves my father has always been supportive of King Charles. I can't wait until our family can be back together."

"I'm happy for you," said Mary in a thin voice as they arrived at the jail and knocked. While they waited for Richard's uncle to open the heavy oak door to let them in, Richard noticed that tears were welling up in Mary's eyes. For some reason, he hadn't thought before about blind people crying. It bothered him deeply.

When Richard and Mary were seated on the straw in the old Bedford jail and John Bunyan had taken the first sips of his noon meal, he leaned back against the stone wall and rubbed his chin. "Last time I told you about how Pilgrim and Hopeful escaped Giant Despair," Bunyan began.

Overhearing that a story was beginning, three other prisoners drifted over and joined them, for there was no privacy in prison, and many had grown to enjoy the preacher's stories. "But this story is about a time when Pilgrim was traveling alone on the road to the Heavenly City." Bunyan paused until everyone was settled. Then he continued.

You know, we cannot always have faithful companions to help us. Even though God gave us the church, we sometimes are alone and must rely on God's other gifts.

For just such a time, Pilgrim had been given the whole armor of God. He had on the breastplate of righteousness and the helmet of salvation. And he carried the shield of faith in one hand and the sword of the Spirit, which is the Word of God, in the other. But there was no armor to protect his back.

So when, one day as he trudged along, he saw a dragon coming toward him over the fields, he knew that he would have to stand his ground. He couldn't turn and run.

This hideous monster was covered with scales like a fish. He had wings like a dragon, feet like a bear, and the head of a lion. Out of his mouth came fire and smoke.

When he had come up to Pilgrim, he looked at him and sneered. "Where do you come from?" the dragon roared. "And where are you headed?"

"I have come from the City of Destruction, and am going to the Heavenly City," answered Pilgrim in a trembling voice. But he did not run!

"Then you are one of my subjects," belched the dragon in a great cloud of black smoke, "for all this country is mine, and I am its prince. Why are you trying to run away from your prince? If I didn't think you could still be of some service to me, I would strike you to the ground this moment with one blow."

"It is true that I was born in your kingdom," said Pilgrim, "but your service was hard, and no one can live on your wages, for it is written, 'The wages of sin is death.' Therefore, when I grew up, I did what any wise person would do. I changed my ways and left your realm."

Dragon snorted. "There is no prince that will lose his subjects so lightly, and neither will I let you go. However," he said, changing his voice to the sweetness of syrup, "since you complain about your service and wages, I'll make you a deal: I hereby promise, if you come back under my rule, I will give you whatever my country can afford."

"But I have promised myself to another," said Pilgrim, "to the King of princes. So how can I, in fairness, go back with you without being hanged as a traitor to Him?"

"You did the same to me," roared Dragon. Then he quieted himself, took a deep breath that sucked all the smoke out of the air around him, and continued in as gentle a voice as his scaly throat could manage. "I am a generous master. Though you have broken your pledge to me, I am willing to forgive all . . . if you will but turn again and come back to me."

Pilgrim sighed. "What I promised you, I

did as a child, and besides, I'm sure the King under whose banner now I stand will forgive me for whatever I did when I was so young. Besides, Dragon, to tell you the truth, I like His service, His wages, His servants, His government, and His company better than yours. Therefore, quit trying to persuade me further. I am His servant, and I will follow Him."

Then Dragon broke out into a monstrous rage, bellowing, "I am an enemy to this King. I hate His person, His laws, and His people. Therefore, I am come out to destroy you!" Two blasts of flame shot from Dragon's nostrils and singed Pilgrim's eyebrows.

"Beware, Dragon, what you do; for I am on the King's highway, the way of holiness, and I am under His protection."

Then the scaly monster straddled the path and said, "I don't care what He might do. Prepare yourself to die, feeble traveler! For I swear by my infernal den, that you shall go no farther. Here I will spill your soul!"

And with that he hurled a flaming dart at Pilgrim's breast. But Pilgrim threw up his shield and deflected it with no harm to himself.

Then Pilgrim drew his sword, for he saw it was time to take the offensive. Dragon lunged at him, firing fiery darts as thick as hail.

Dodging and weaving and using his shield to every advantage, Pilgrim fended off the darts, but his efforts were not perfect and three missiles got through his defenses to wound him in his head, his hand, and his foot.

Seeing Pilgrim fall back a little, Dragon followed up his attack with even greater fury. But Pilgrim did not lose heart and rallied his courage to resist as manfully as he could.

This fierce combat lasted for half a day until Pilgrim was almost exhausted. For his wounds caused him to grow weaker and weaker.

Then Dragon, seeing his opportunity, moved in on Pilgrim and, wrestling him tooth and nail, gave him a dreadful fall. Pilgrim landed so hard that his sword flew out of his hand.

"Ah-ha," roared Dragon, "I have you now," and leaped upon him to crush him to death. The weight of the foul-smelling beast was so great that Pilgrim thought he was done for.

But just as Dragon was rising to deliver his last blow, Pilgrim stretched out his hand for his sword and caught it, saying, "Don't count me out yet, you rotten brute. For though I fall, I shall arise again." Then Pilgrim gave him a deadly thrust, which made Dragon fall back as though he had received his mortal wound. Seeing his advantage, Pilgrim made at him again with his sword, saying, "It is written that 'in all these things we are more than conquerors through Him that loved us.'"

And with that, Dragon spread his leathery wings and with much flapping and wheezing managed to rise unsteadily into the air. Pilgrim watched as the smoldering monster careened over the fields until he was no more than an oily smudge against the evening's sunset, never to trouble Pilgrim again.

But from this battle, Pilgrim learned one lesson. Never again did he go about with his sword in its sheath. For as the Scriptures say, "The Word of God is quick, and powerful, and sharper than any two-edged sword."

"Hear, hear," cheered the prisoners who had gathered around to hear the story. "Very good. Very good."

"You ought to put those stories in a book," said Richard as he stood up.

"Oh, I don't know," laughed the preacher. "I'm glad you like them, but what good would it do to write them down?" Then he also stood and dusted his hands off. "Well, it's probably time for you to get down to the Swan to catch your coach." He clapped Richard's shoulders with his hands. "May God go with you, my boy, and don't forget to stand your ground. Things look cheery today, but life will bring its troubles. Remember to use your Sword!"

In a matter of moments, Richard's uncle had opened the doors and was waving good-bye to him as he went on his way. But as the boy trudged down the dusty street of Bedford toward the Swan Inn, he couldn't help wondering, *What kind of a man is this John Bunyan who has found such peace in jail?*

He thought about the two men he knew best who were in prison: his father, a political prisoner; the other, a simple preacher who told stories. One would soon be free; the other would remain behind bars simply because of his convictions.

I wonder, Richard thought, turning back to look at the Bedford county jail, *what kind of a man will I become?*

More About John Bunyan

John Bunyan was born in 1628 in the small town of Elstow, near Bedford, in southern England. He was the son of a tinker, someone who repaired pots and pans, sharpened knives, and did other metal work that did not require a large forge. Such a trade—and the necessary tools—was passed down from generation to generation.

On his sixteenth birthday, Bunyan reported for duty in the parliamentary army. Though he did not have strong political views, this did pit him against King Charles I. In about 1648 he married. Some think his wife was called Mary, after whom their first child was named, but that is uncertain. Daughter Mary was born blind and received John's deep tenderness and affection.

John's wife was a Puritan and inspired within John a powerful religious conversion. This led to his becoming a lay preacher in the nonconformist congregations of Bedford.

His style was powerful and direct, and he became a favorite preacher in the surrounding towns. However, except for the rise of nonconformist churches under the rule of Oliver Cromwell, it was unheard of for a lowly tinker to presume to preach. And once the monarchy was restored, the government did everything it could to stamp out these independent churches and preachers.

John's first wife died in about 1658 after bearing four children. As someone who thrived on married life, this left him devastated and in need of help in raising four small children, the oldest of whom was only eight years old and blind. Within a year John married Elizabeth, who some have suggested was John's much younger second cousin and thereby knew John and the children well.

Whatever the case, she became a devoted wife and mother and bore two more children. Throughout his life, she loyally supported him and his ministry.

In the meantime, big changes had been happening on the political front. In 1640, the English Revolution had erupted in the form of a series of political alliances and bloody battles essentially between King Charles I's army and the parliament's army, the one into which John Bunyan and most young men in his county had been recruited. For ten years the civil war raged back and forth, pitting family against family and town against town. Loyalties frequently changed, and just as frequently treason was charged.

Finally, the parliamentary army won, essentially under the leadership of Oliver Cromwell. The monarchy was suspended, Charles I having been executed, and reforms were instituted, loosing the grip the Church of England had on the common people.

Oliver Cromwell emerged from the warfare and political turmoil as the Lord Protector of England and a powerful ruler for the next eight years.

As a devout Puritan, he allowed religious freedom for Puritans, Quakers, Baptists, Presbyterians, and other nonconformists. Several Anglican bishops (many of whom had sided with the king during the civil war) were removed from office, and some churches fell into the hands of the nonconformists. "Religion of the people" spread like revival. It was this populist movement that gave John Bunyan the chance to become a preacher.

Of course, all this change made enemies of many powerful people who waited for the day when they could turn the tables and return to power.

When Cromwell died on September 3, 1658, the country drifted toward anarchy under his inept son, Richard, until General George Monck, commander of the army of Scotland, invaded England, marching all the way into London in February 1660. The revolution was over.

General Monck recalled the Long Parliament, and it then contacted Charles II, who had been in exile on the continent in the town of Breda, Netherlands. In April 1660, in a proclamation known as the Declaration of Breda, Charles II promised that if Parliament allowed him to return to the throne, he would accept a parliamentary form of government and grant amnesty to his enemies. He was brought back to England and finally restored to the throne on May 8, 1660.

He did not, however, keep his promise, and soon simple preachers as well as actual political enemies were being thrown in prison all over the country. In fairness to Charles II, there was an active revolutionary group afoot that he had reason to fear. They called themselves the Fifth Monarchy and wanted to throw out the king and establish a government under "King Jesus" with, of course, themselves in charge.

The specific reason John Bunyan was jailed involved his preaching without a license. Of course, being a nonconformist, he could not get a license even though he had pastored a church for several years. As this story shows, the details of the arrest and sentencing were legally questionable, and Bunyan had good reason to petition for a new trial.

During his first few months in prison, John White, his jailer, often allowed him out on informal parole to attend services. And on one occasion, Bunyan even went to London. Then the magistrates cracked down, and he spent most of the next twelve years in the Bedford county jail.

Near the end of his time there, he probably wrote the majority of his masterpiece, *Pilgrim's Progress*, as well as several other tracts and books. He was released in 1672 and returned to his life as a pastor. However, his writings, which finally numbered more than sixty books, caused him to be much in demand as a preacher all over southern England.

He died in London in 1688 from pneumonia, which he apparently caught after riding far out of his way through a chilling rainstorm to help settle a quarrel between a father and son.

For Further Reading

Brittain, Vera Mary. *Valiant Pilgrim, the Story of John Bunyan and Puritan England*. New York: Macmillan, 1950.

Bunyan, John. *Pilgrim's Progress*. London: J. M. Dent & Sons, 1962 (the public domain edition from which scenes were adapted for this book).

Hill, Christopher. *A Tinker and a Poor Man*. New York: Knopf, 1989.

Talon, Henri. *John Bunyan, the Man and His Works*. Cambridge, Mass.: Harvard University Press, 1951.

Venables, Edmund. *Life of John Bunyan*. London: Walter Scott, 1888.

Winslow, Ola Elizabeth. *John Bunyan*. New York: Macmillan, 1961.